T0008718

"Christine Estima's debut is startling and heartrending, generous and vivid. It's easy to fall in love with Christine's insistence on compassion for women who were afforded little of it. With extraordinary prose and boundless empathy, *The Syrian Ladies Benevolent Society* asks us to consider if we are inevitable products of our family history. No matter what answer you land on, this book will transform you."

—Elamin Abdelmahmoud, author of *Son of Elsewhere*

"In *The Syrian Ladies Benevolent Society*, the past is very much a living character that shapes and informs the present moment. Christine Estima has penned a refreshingly vibrant and multicultural portrait of Montreal that braids together different branches of the historical record with precise prose and a sharp eye for human complexity."

—Dimitri Nasrallah, author of *Hotline*

"Vivid and arresting from the very first line, this accomplished debut will leave an indelible imprint on your heart and mind with its powerful prose and compassionate storytelling. This collection weaves women together through the fabric of time— and through their bravery, humanity, and hope even in the face of atrocities and defeat. Compulsively readable and intricately wrought, *The Syrian Ladies Benevolent Society* is a must-read from a writer to watch."

—Marissa Stapley, *New York Times*–bestselling author of *Lucky*

"Gorgeous and gutting, *The Syrian Ladies Benevolent Society* asks (screams, whispers): What makes us? Are we our pasts, all our histories and families and generational traumas stacked on top of each other like a piece of additive sculpture? Or are we our present, our choices, remaking ourselves each day in a continual act of becoming? Instead of answering with either/or, this book says (screams, whispers), over and over again, yes."

—Natalie Zina Walschots, author of *Hench*

THE SYRIAN LADIES BENEVOLENT SOCIETY

CHRISTINE ESTIMA

Published in Canada in 2023 and the USA in 2023 by House of Anansi Press Inc.
houseofanansi.com

House of Anansi Press is committed to protecting our natural environment.
This book is made of material from well-managed FSC®-certified forests, recycled materials,
and other controlled sources.

House of Anansi Press is a Global Certified Accessible™ (GCA by Benetech) publisher.
The ebook version of this book meets stringent accessibility standards and is available
to readers with print disabilities.

27 26 25 24 23   1 2 3 4 5

Library and Archives Canada Cataloguing in Publication
Title: The Syrian ladies benevolent society / Christine Estima.
Names: Estima, Christine, author.
Identifiers: Canadiana (print) 20230452000 | Canadiana (ebook) 2023045206X | ISBN
9781487012335 (softcover) | ISBN 9781487012342 (EPUB)
Classification: LCC PS8609.S75 S97 2023 | DDC C813/.6—dc23

Book design: Lucia Kim
Cover image: *Anna* by Meaghan Ogilvie

*House of Anansi Press is grateful for the privilege to work on and create from the Traditional Territory
of many Nations, including the Anishinabeg, the Wendat, and the Haudenosaunee, as well as the Treaty
Lands of the Mississaugas of the Credit.*

Canada Council   Conseil des Arts
for the Arts   du Canada

ONTARIO ARTS COUNCIL
CONSEIL DES ARTS DE L'ONTARIO
an Ontario government agency
un organisme du gouvernement de l'Ontario

With the participation of the Government of Canada
Avec la participation du gouvernement du Canada

*We acknowledge for their financial support of our publishing program the Canada Council for the Arts,
the Ontario Arts Council, and the Government of Canada.*

Printed and bound in Canada

MIX
Paper from
responsible sources
FSC® C103567

For Sito
Louise Zarbatany
1922–2016

Content note: While this book has been written with care for its readers and characters alike, it does contend with violent themes that should be approached with caution. There are stories in this collection that contain references to self-harm, domestic violence, sexual assault, xenophobia, racism, warfare, and queerphobia. Take care when reading.

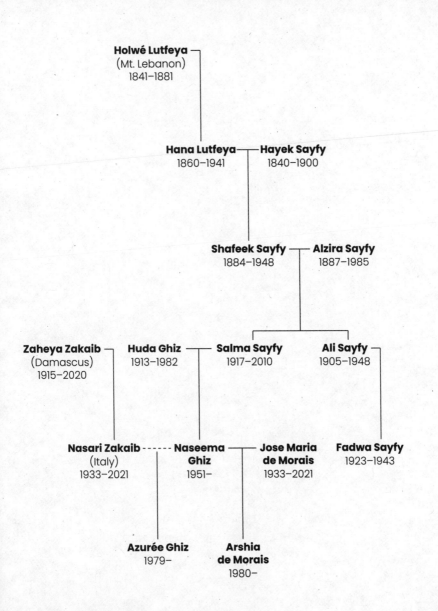

CONTENTS

PART ONE

My heart was hot within me,
while I was musing the fire burned.

Psalm 39:3

THE CASTLE OF MONTREAL

1860

WHEN THEY BROKE DOWN the door, I was already crouching in the field. It smelled like cow shit and burnt hay. Hana was bundled and slung across my chest. Her breath was warm like the cinders in the air. I knew the Druze would come. The village whispers said they were in the next town over. I saw the church burn from here. The whispers said they ran the Father through. They wore red sashes.

Elamin the Beetle was the biggest whisperer. "Let me tell you what I saw in Rashaya al-Wadi. They enucleated the eyes of the priest and doused the congregation in burning oil!"

Elamin had a full name, to be sure, but he was always known as the Beetle to us, and I cannot remember from where the name came, or if it ever left him. Elamin the Beetle grabbed every person in the village by the arm and shook them with worry, but somehow, our doubt was thicker than papyrus stalks. The children continued to go to school, the butcher hung a fresh cow head at his stall every morning, the woven bushels of rice and cardamom husks weighed down each braying donkey's spine.

Elamin the Beetle grew angrier the more he was questioned about what he saw. "If you have truth on your side, why do you care if you're not believed?"

He had no answer.

I will never know why his eyes horrified me like two black swirls in a tar pit, but something told me to believe him.

My house was mud-brick, some stone, with interlocking wood beams. I watched it burn like brimstone. I gave Hana water with aniseed, sweet like licorice, so she wouldn't cry.

The men in the sashes went from my house to the next—it, too, disappeared in the fire. The embers burned my throat. The unmistakable sound of women screaming, and then suddenly going quiet, before low moaning, came from every house.

I tightened Hana's sling and ran in the night. The air always blows toward the shoreline in the early hours, so I followed it. Every donkey stable or chicken coop along the way was empty. A woman's sandal lay in a pile of feed.

When the Druze in their sashes came over the hills, Elamin the Beetle hollered, "I told you so all along!" I managed to get away, but only God knows where the Beetle finds himself now. Or if his warnings were worth it.

The dead lay at the side of the road, their bodies left in the midday sun. Even at such a late hour, the stench lingered, like a hog with maggots eating its putrid hoof. There was a line of carts on the road, all without a donkey or a horse. The moonlight moved quietly over them; the wind barely rattled them.

BEFORE THE CALL to prayer echoed at dawn, I came across some elderly men and children. We huddled together in a coal cellar. "There's not enough help for us," the old men said, explaining the French expeditionary forces were overwhelmed with refugees. The Belgian, too, some said. If we could make it to Beirut, maybe, but that meant days on foot, eating wild dates that gave us the shits, and maybe scarabs.

Hana was only six months old, but she remained quiet if she was up against my skin. During the night treks, with the bruised sky looming over us, she never made a sound. I stole clothes from a line when her sling ripped. I didn't feel guilty. During the day, men roamed with pistols. So, I kept low and tried to breastfeed. Inshallah, I still had the milk within me.

I cried as Hana slept. Not because I was sad, but because she wasn't. She didn't know her father. The night before the Druze invaded, the village whispers said he was already dead. He went to fight when he heard crosses were being drawn on the streets so Christian symbols would be desecrated, either by feet or horse shit.

Hana suckled and gurgled with a light in her eye, unaware that we brought this upon ourselves. That's what the old men said to me when they realized I'm of the lineage of betrayal. It had been my family, almost a thousand years ago, that helped the French who came on their horses with their flags, their chain-mail suits of armour sizzling in the sun. They built a fortress high on the crests of the hills when their greatest threat was the Kurdish sultan. The land was holy, but the French were not, and they came back bloody year after bloody year. It was said the Kurdish sultan besieged their castle for two years. When the French lost, they escaped through a secret stairwell that flowed down to the catacombs with the help of the locals. The locals were my blood. The town was called Shobak. The French castle was called Montreal. The royal mountain.

By the third night on foot, our group of old men and young children was noticeably smaller. If dysentery prevented them from keeping up with the pack, they fell where they defecated. One man's foot twisted in a grouse hole. The imams at the mosques chastised us for using the fields as latrines and wouldn't let us sleep inside, the dusk call to prayer telling us to move on. We walked at night, as we couldn't afford to be seen in daylight.

"In Beirut, there are ships," the children said. They told these stories to each other like schoolroom gossip. "The ships are big, and there's room for everyone! They take you where the Druze cannot go."

One boy, who saw Hana suckling on my breast, said he could grant me passage on a ship if I let him suckle, too. A good smack was what he needed. He stood there in a puddle of midnight black from the rains and held his cheek like a cormorant with a bruised wing.

The call to prayer became a marker. Time to rise, time to rest, time to walk, time to sleep. The chant never bothered me before, but then I felt its serpentine melody in my bones. The voice echoing from the minaret would strike me, ricochet inside me, before the final note broke off. Hana wouldn't latch. My milk started to dry up. One old man found me some mint and grapes to chew. "For the baby," he said. I thanked him but didn't see him the next evening as the group began to march. The others said he ventured off to find me shelled nuts. We couldn't afford to wait for him before moving on. I wondered if the men with pistols found him.

The other old men could not be trusted. Hana began to cry during the day, cold and hungry, unable to sleep. The elders' grunts turned to swats from their canes. They swatted to scare her, to scare me, but they wouldn't dare strike. *They should know better than to come for an infant, surely.* I rocked her in my arms, quietly begging, "Hana, my baby, don't you cry, Hana my baby, don't you cry."

When she finally slept, I could not. Thoughts tortured me: *How did I get us here? What have I done? Look at what I have caused.* Thoughts that didn't seem to even come from inside me, like they belonged to someone else, and were meant to drive me mad. The wind jeered. I crawled with Hana underneath the wooden carts left abandoned on the road and tried to stow away from the blazing midday sun. But the dusk was also intense, the rain keen.

WE KNEW WE were close to Beirut; we could smell it upstream. Cities are like this, with everyone emptying their chamber pots into the streets, the vermin and insects feeding off one another, and entire stables of asses defecating near wells. Perhaps only one night was left until we reached the city walls.

I awoke that evening ready to pull my daughter into her sling, her tiny wet mouth and soft cheeks peeking out, and carry her to safety. But there was a blunt mark on her back, a lump of red flesh. Screaming from under the wooden cart, I looked up to see the old men.

Some avoided my glare; some raised their fists to me.

"You, your baby, you are both curses to us!"

"Take your demon child away!"

"The cries, they are the cries of the damned. God will have his vengeance!"

I grabbed my Hana and ran along the coastline, south to Beirut. Hana was alive, but her cries were floating inside her like a white dandelion on the wind. Nausea hit me swiftly. Her cries, the horror.

The night turned soft and black. I ran until my breath turned to acid. Hana's cries were like droplets in the water, rippling. *Maybe there are ships in Beirut. Maybe the children were right.*

When I was a little girl, my mother and father buried a baby. A brother, I was supposed to have, but he didn't live long after the moment light touched him. The local priest cut out the heart of my brother and placed glowing embers in his empty cavity. As he lay in the earth, all we could see was a shining red glow coming from his tiny body. His ribs turned black, charred, before the priest wrapped him in cloth and closed the grave.

"Hana, my baby, do not cry." I rocked my daughter. "Hana, my baby, hush or die."

MY SANDALS TORE from my feet at dawn as I neared the gates of Beirut. The city walls rose higher than the prayer chant from the minaret, the muezzin's voice light. Pigeons marched like small infantries up and down the stone streets, demanding scraps of bread and nuts. Hana guzzled the air; so much so, the men guarding the gates took pity and called for her care.

I was brought to the home of a wet nurse, who had skin the colour of raw meat and hair that scraggled down her forehead. I was intimidated by the respect commanded by her simple entrance. A swagger that denoted her queendom, while I was clearly a serf. But Hana's cheeks were filled, finally! I, too, drank milk, with oil of rose petals and honey nectar, chewed a handful of almonds, and smoked a pipe of snuff.

"There are ships," the wet nurse said, her eyes blank, Hana grasping her blouse. The children were correct. "But if you want passage, you have to satisfy the Ottomans."

"How do I do that?"

"For a woman, the options are customarily either giving your body or serving their empire," she said, pulling my daughter back from her dripping brown nipple, fastening the clip on her blouse. Handing me my child, she said she had a connection, so I begged for a meeting. I had some silver akçe coins but not enough to pay her, so she told me to go milk her donkey, and then return that evening.

I was happy to do the work, but when I returned, I asked why the donkey's milk?

"One day my breast will dry up like yours. I wouldn't want that to affect business."

"Donkey's milk might kill an infant," I replied.

"Is that so?" she said, inspecting the terracotta jar I had filled for her. She didn't have anything else to say after that. The wet nurse could not be trusted, just like the elderly men, and the children in the pack. I left with my baby.

But then, as I walked through the narrow streets and the sky above me glowed with the warm tones of dusk, I saw the city for what it was. Men pissed in doorways, smoking and arguing, and horse excrement steamed in the lanes. Women sold their bodies to men with irascible, bitter coughs and unshaven beards. Crowds of gaunt, waiflike figures had gathered near the old tower to watch the guards hang the body of a convicted thief from the city walls, a thin trail of blood from her nose and a look of surprise stained on her face.

BEFORE DUSK FELL, I returned to the wet nurse with my daughter to find two men in crimson fez hats inside her home. They gave me new sandals, a clean head scarf, and a cold pistol.

"Find a way to smuggle this past the French expeditionary forces to the Turks on the ships," they said, "and there will be rewards."

The iron gun in my hand had no handle. The zarbatan, they called it. With a breath from my lips, the victim would be shot and killed.

"What are the Turks doing on the ships?"

"Departing for Constantinople," the men in hats said.

The wet nurse shooed them out of her quarters and grabbed my arm. "Be wary of anyone who promises rewards," she whispered. "Including God."

"What have you heard?"

"If you get on the ships with the Turks, don't disembark at Constantinople, lest you be mistaken for an enemy and slaughtered where you stand," she said, as she grabbed a hunk of coal and some logs to make up a fire for her copper cauldron. "The journey is long; the ships will make many stops. Constantinople is only the first. They refuel, and then carry on to Genoa, and other ports along the sea." She motioned for me to follow her outside to the sunken well where she filled her bucket.

"Where might we go then?"

"My advice? Go back to where you came from."

"We cannot. The Druze are in every corner. They burned down my village."

"Then stay on the ship. They eventually cross the ocean to the Province of Canada."

I'd never heard of this place. She explained it was vast, lush. She had helped others escape to its shores and leave behind this land of flies and dirt.

The place to disembark, she said, was called Montreal.

My body seized at the name, and my grip on the pistol tightened until my palms shook.

"Why is it called that?" I asked.

"The French—" she swatted the air. "Once they were everywhere. Once they ruled the world. Now they beg for their former slaves to populate their colonies."

I didn't dare say a word about my family. It was one thing to admit my family were traitors; it was another thing altogether to admit I, too, was a traitor. I would always be a traitor. But powerful men line their pockets and their coffers every day with the blood of my people. Why not a woman?

The wet nurse gave a big heave on the well latch and water spurted forth.

"Why are you helping me?" I asked after a moment.

She lifted the bucket and met my eye. "I'm not. May you live, or may you die; only God cares for such details. But to help your infant daughter, that is of value to me."

"How so?"

"Have you ever buried a child and set their heart cavity aflame?" she asked.

I thought of my brother, his rib bones black. "Yes."

She said her breast was wet because she, too, had a child. They couldn't escape the city, and the infant died. "I don't know you, and I don't care to. But no mother should be left alone in a country like this, all alone with nothing but coal where her heart used to be."

I thought of Elamin the Beetle. When no one heeded

his warnings, he cried, "There is more to lose than just your way!"

I had lost everything except the gun and my child. Maybe in Montreal, I thought, I could glow from the inside again, replacing my burnt heart.

THE NIGHT SET IN, gusty, with dark clouds bundling up from the west. Now and then, a growl of thunder or a flash of lightning foretold that a dust storm was close. The steel beasts were docked along La Corniche, their bellies full of families leaving this bleating heat behind.

A few horse carriages pulled up to the docks, and women who still had a bloom to their faces emerged, flashed their documents to the French, and then moved to the ships. Men with hunched backs and shirts ripped at the collar carried the ladies' valises on their backs across the boarding plank.

With Hana slung on my back, I tucked the dismantled pistol inside her bundle. The coolness of its metal would keep her sleeping. I approached the docks, and the French forces.

Something hot and squealing buzzed over my shoulder. Suddenly there was a lot of screaming.

Pistol blasts whizzed from behind me, and a few French soldiers fell like heavy stones. Gunfire crossed and everyone scattered. I'd never heard anything so loud. Louder than the waves crashing against the hulls, or the shearing violence of a dust tornado. Blood and skulls crashed about our feet. The Druze. It had to be. Another terror, another skirmish; they were all meant for me. Small children ran clutching their father's hand; women fell where they stood, their bundles splayed like fish. Bodies were ripped apart; the skin burned while their oils evaporated.

I ran in the direction of the ships, clopping across the boarding plank while men with coal staining their faces screamed from below to retreat from the waters. Hana bobbed on my back, her eyes shaken open and her cries louder than the blasts. I was alive, my child was alive, and we had a pistol.

On the deck, I pulled on Hana's sling until she slid into my arms. Reaching for the dismantled zarbatan, I twisted the barrel into place and dropped in a pellet from the bandolier. The men in the red sashes were advancing from La Corniche down to the slips with daggers in their eyes, so I drew a big gulp of air and put my lips to the apparatus. I shot a man in the foot, taking his toe clean off. Hot tears speckled my face as he screamed. The zarbatan was searing hot and hissing, like the blood in my veins.

The plank was hoisted and the ship's engines reversed from shore. When I finally found a quiet corner in the lower decks to huddle for the journey, I felt my breast swelling. Bringing Hana close to my skin, I watched her face, her small eyes blinking. Her two lips and tongue flattened against me, suckling. She closed her eyes. I imagined the warmth of my milk soothing her stomach, calming her nerves. She gripped onto my blouse, her fat fingers in a fist, and then looked up at me again, like she could forgive our betrayals, past and present.

THE SYRIAN LADIES
BENEVOLENT SOCIETY

1934

SAYFY FELT THE COTTON on the gingham dress flounce over the nylons, and a rush of appreciation surged. The Peter Pan neckline with a faint glimmer of pearls above it, the curve of the dress as it draped the hips, the empire waist, the subtle crescent moon that the sheer nylons made along the calf, leading down to the brogue penny loafers; it was so modern and besotting. And the red gloves hid Sayfy's rough and callused hands.

Behind the delicate stained oak folding partition in the dressing room, Sayfy admired all that was reflected in the mirror, illuminated by the faintest morning light beyond the window drapes.

A loud knock at the dressing room door knocked Sayfy out of the trance.

"How are you finding everything, sir?" the salesgirl called out from the department store floor.

Shafeek Sayfy immediately grabbed the dress's hemline and flung it up and over his head. He unclipped the nylons from the garter belt, unbelted the garter from his waist, and folded the gloves inside the glove box.

"Yes, I will be taking the tie!" he called out, retrieving the tie from the chair in the corner, as he quickly put his trousers on and hoisted them up with the suspenders, clipping his pinky finger and stifling a yelp.

"And I do believe my wife will very much enjoy this dress," he hollered, slipping into his vest and watch fob. "Can you wrap them for me?"

"Of course, sir. I will meet you at the register desk."

Fumbling with the buttons on his collar, Sayfy took one last look at himself in the mirror, licking his fingers to smooth his hair, and then repeating the process for the generous eyebrows that burned a hirsute path across his brow.

Taking a breath, he emerged from the dressing room and carried the garments to the desk. He fumbled with his chequebook as the salesgirl folded the tie, the dress, the nylons, the garter belt, and the gloves into tissue paper and boxes.

She peered up from her handiwork and gave him a curious look, her eyes lingering just below his lips for a moment too long. Sayfy felt heat rise in his cheeks.

"Whom shall I make the cheque out to, my dear?" He

layered the charm thick, even adding a two-percent tip for her troubles after she organized the delivery of goods for later that evening.

It was only once he was outside on Avenue Henri-Julien and caught a glimpse of himself in the shop window that he realized the pearls were still around his neck, peeking not so subtly out from his collar.

Making a mental note never to return to that shop ever again (unless, that is, to burn it down to the ground), he tucked the necklace behind his collar and dashed across Jean Talon until he reached Saint-Dominique. He climbed up to the third floor of the corner building and swung open the door to the meeting already in progress.

"Ah, Shaf, you're back," Mrs. Boutarah said at the head of the boardroom, shuffling her foolscap on the table. "Lose your way, did you?"

Eyeing him from the table were ten women, all wives of prominent men in the community, and all entirely sick of his tardiness and excuses.

"Thank you for waiting." He pulled up his collar and yanked out a seat. "I wouldn't want to miss the opportunity to edit the monthly newsletter."

Mrs. Boutarah, Mrs. Salhani, Mrs. Bouassaly, Mrs. Zakaib, Mrs. Ayoub, Mrs. Khoury, Mrs. Saad, Mrs. Ghiz, and Mrs. Nassif made up the Syrian Ladies Benevolent Society, established in 1905 and a pillar in the community of Arabs populating Montreal's Little Italy. Sayfy, the lone pigeon among the cats, was serving as alternate supervisor in the absence of the priest, whose duties for the church took him away from these meetings. Sayfy wasn't entirely sure why a ladies' society needed male supervision, but he also didn't understand the point of a church solely for Arabs. Then again, if the Church of England could do it, why not they?

The new recording secretary, a young unmarried woman, sat in the corner and began jotting down notes even before the meeting was called to order.

"So you're the new minute taker?" he said.

"Yes," she yipped nervously, and he figured he was the first person in the room to acknowledge her. "Mr. Sayfy, my name is Miss Saykaly, and my mother helped me to join. I'm very happy to be here, and I hope I can be of help."

Mrs. Boutarah interjected loudly from across the table, "Yes, Miss Saykaly would be a lovely creature if she could grow legs."

Miss Saykaly froze and stared straight ahead. Sayfy thought of the department store fitting room, how quiet and peaceful it was, and wished he were still locked behind its doors.

"Shaf, if you please." Mrs. Boutarah gestured to his empty seat, and he obliged her by taking it. Beyond the window, on a tree bough, a squirrel was hissing at a pigeon, ready to fight.

The meeting over the latest benevolent society

newsletter dragged on, and Sayfy couldn't imagine how Miss Saykaly could possibly keep up with all these minutes that were now lost to the ravages of time. Minutes he would never get back. He pulled up his collar, even though he was sweating like a Protestant in confession.

Mrs. Boutarah's voice cut into his daydream. "Shaf! Why did you change that word?" she blurted out, tapping the draft several times for effect. He glanced through the documents before him, realizing she was referencing an alteration to her text about the holy Church of Antioch.

Outside the meeting room, a telephone rang, and Miss Saykaly quickly exited.

As Mrs. Boutarah looked at him menacingly down her spectacles, Sayfy replied, "Well, it's the verb, and it didn't agree with the subject. So, I made them agree."

She looked to the heavens, as if Jesus cared for grammatical errors. "Does it have to agree?"

Sayfy felt a familiar tense heat brewing in his rib cage. "It's church policy that they do."

"Well," she tossed the limp pages back down onto the table, "that shows an exceptional lack of imagination."

"If it's imagination you want, join the Mormon Church," he muttered.

Miss Saykaly poked her head back in. "Telephone call for you, Mr. Sayfy."

"Who is it?"

"Oh. I didn't ask. Shall I do that now?"

Sayfy got to his feet with a big harrumph. "My dear, you must always announce a telephone caller. One always wants to know to whom one is speaking."

"I didn't want to pry, sir."

Sayfy pushed through the door and picked up the receiver, but not before telling Miss Saykaly, "Then you're in the wrong congregation."

Miss Saykaly blinked. Somewhere outside on the street below a car screeched to a halt.

"Hello?"

"Papa!"

"Salma. What's the matter?"

"Can you come to Madame Dineen's Boutique on Saint-Hubert, next to the Théâtre Plaza?"

Sayfy sighed and tugged on his pearls. Salma was affianced, and the big day was quickly approaching. But Salma kept flip-flopping between gown styles, and Madame Dineen had expressed that choices needed to be made in order to complete the dress before showtime. The thought of having to shop again with his indecisive daughter didn't appeal to Sayfy.

Then again, any excuse to remove himself from the gaggle of non-benevolent benevolent ladies...

"I'll be there before quarter past," he said, grabbing his overcoat and scarf from the rack and refusing to say good-bye to the ladies in the meeting.

It was November, still sunny and above the seasonal temperature, as he ran across Jean Talon, keeping his eyes lowered as he passed Henri-Julien for fear of bumping into the salesgirl from the morning, and dashed down Saint-Hubert. Little flakes of snow had swirled about the sky that morning but hadn't collected once they hit the ground. Still, this was Montreal; if it doesn't call for snow, bring galoshes anyway.

As Sayfy pushed through the glass door of Madame Dineen's Boutique, which also sold hats and stoles, the door chime announced him before he could. Salma and Madame Dineen were in the back; they both raised their faces as he approached.

"Papa!" Salma flung her arms around him.

"What is it, my darling? Hold on, let me look at you."

Salma took a step back, wearing a flower-trimmed silk gown with an empire waist that hugged her torso and hips, all the way down to her knees, where it finally flowed outward. The V-shaped décolletage made a hearty meal of her collarbones, and the veil gauzed her pencil-thin eyebrows, which were de rigueur among young women.

"Do you like it? It's just like the gown Claudette Colbert wore in *It Happened One Night!*" she said.

"Wasn't that the picture where Clark Gable didn't wear an undershirt?"

"Papa, you focus on all the wrong details."

Sayfy took off his scarf and overcoat and handed them

to Madame Dineen, who placed them in the courtesy wardrobe. He made sure to pull up his collar once again.

"Why, Madame Dineen," he said, taking her by the hand, "what happened to your sapphire cocktail ring?"

"Ah ouais," she said in her thick joual accent. "I lose it."

"Heartbreaking! Where did you lose it?"

"In a . . . comment dit-on . . . in a buttercream custard."

"I beg your pardon?"

"This has happen before," she shrugged, leaving him entirely bewildered.

"Now, Papa," Salma began, taking him by the hand, "what do you think? Should Madame Dineen embroider beads along the neckline? Or perhaps we should stay with the floral design and add a layer of lace."

It was impossible for Sayfy to comprehend how the girl who was born exactly three years to the day after the Archduke Ferdinand was assassinated in Sarajevo could already be encumbered with such adult decisions. Wasn't it just yesterday that she used to call out to him late at night so that they might sit by her window alcove together and watch the rain streak patterns downward? He would pick one drop, she would pick another, and they would pretend it was a race down to the pane.

"I think you look entirely too spectacular for words right now, darling. You shouldn't change a thing."

"Papa." She smirked at him before turning to show him

the back of the dress, which was clipped up and down. "This is just a sample dress. Madame Dineen needs to fashion mine to my size and taste."

"Ah, I see. Well, why don't you ask Huda?" He liked Salma's intended bridegroom; he was quiet, unobtrusive, and enjoyed his privacy, much like Sayfy.

"Huda? He wouldn't know a dress from a doorstop!"

Salma spun around again to look at herself in the cheval mirror. She smoothed her gloved fingers over her hips, and Sayfy envisioned himself in such finery. He shivered a little and pulled up his collar once more.

"I just want the wedding ceremony to be perfect," she sighed. "Let's not forget..."

Sayfy knew exactly why she trailed off. The showroom floor fell silent with the memory. Mrs. Zakaib had sold her daughter, Maryam, into marriage in utero, and earlier this year she was wed at the age of twelve. The night of her union with Jamal Hayek, she wanted to play with her dolls, but Hayek had other ideas. When she threw a fit as he took away her toys, his temper flared. He strangled her just before the point of death, and then beat her with a belt. That was in March. Now, in early November, thirteen-year-old Maryam was expecting, and soon.

The priest, the congregation, the community, the entire Syrian Ladies Benevolent Society, and even Mrs. Zakaib herself refused to call this an obscene tragedy. It made Sayfy sick, and the collective silence made Sayfy hate the priest's divine responsibilities. *Putting "Father" or "Reverend" before your name is not substantial enough an achievement,* he had thought to himself at the time. Not if your morals stink like rotting offal.

At the thought of something similar ever happening to his daughter, intense heat in his chest constricted his breathing, and he put his hand to his throat. Swallowing hard, Sayfy tugged his collar up again for good measure.

"Shall we make order now, Monsieur?" Madame Dineen said, with her ledger and pencil in hand.

"Salma?" Sayfy directed Madame Dineen's question to her.

"Yes, let's!" she said. "And, Papa, you really have to nudge Ali about getting his suit tailored. He is procrastinating for far too long on it."

Ah yes, Ali, Sayfy thought of his son, *the cobbler who would be a milkman.* Why on earth Ali wanted to give up a dependable and honourable profession like tending to the leather and soles of boots and shoes for delivering the juice from a bovine's teat every morning was beyond him. His chest pain flickered.

Madame Dineen scribbled the invoice on the ledger and shoved the pencil back into her bee's nest of hair. "Alors, that come to twenty dollars."

"Twenty!" Sayfy exclaimed. "Does the dress open up into a pied-à-terre on Côte-Saint-Luc?"

"The times, Monsieur." Madame Dineen looked down her spectacles at him. "Blame the times."

"Papa," Salma cautioned, "I really want this one."

Sayfy couldn't believe this depression, or recession, or whatever the wireless news source was calling it, could drive prices up so astronomically. Since long before the Great War, Sayfy had done quite well for himself selling life insurance. Hell, he even had the good sense to buy war bonds that paid off once the boys came home. The thirties, however, made a monkey out of him. He flattered himself by thinking he wasn't near destitution like other families on his street, but during the lean moments when insurance wasn't a hot commodity, he had secretly sold some of his wife's jewellery. He dreaded the day she would notice.

"Think of it this way, Monsieur Sayfy," Madame Dineen offered. "I want you to look around this room and contemplate: every one of these people went into shop in which other clothes were available and instead selected what they wearing en ce moment précis."

Sayfy's wife, Alzira, had selected his pinstriped shirt from a shop in which other things were definitely available, so he wondered, looking down at himself, if he passed the test. He pulled up his collar once more.

"Exactly!" Salma said. "We want to make an impression. Please, Papa?"

Sayfy sighed, thinking of his purchase that morning. A man should always be in a financial position to throw money at his problems, he reasoned, but sometimes the problems wanted a refund. Once again, he pulled out his chequebook.

"We also have to organize a photographer for the nuptial announcement in the *Gazette*," Salma said, as she and Sayfy bundled up in their coats. His chest did a flip and a thud.

As they pushed through the door with the chime, Madame Dineen called over their shoulders, "N'oubliez pas! Wear the simplest thing you can when having photo taken. It either a photo of your face or your clothes, but it cannot be both!"

Sayfy felt the tension in his chest intensify with her parting words, and as they stepped outside, the incredible winter gales that had for so long stayed away suddenly descended upon Little Italy. The flakes of snow that earlier weren't sticking now clung to their scarves and eyebrows. Black glazed ice appeared, and like clockwork, the bad weather encouraged motorists to forget their training.

The queue for the city bus grew longer than the frequency of buses. Father and daughter were bad-tempered waiting in the bitter cold that stung their skin, as was everyone else. Salma yammered on about how thoughtful Huda was, and how pleased she was to have him as her future husband, while Sayfy pondered how he was going to afford this monstrous wedding. How he shouldn't have foolishly spent that money that morning. How he was certain he once saw Huda flipping up the collar of his trench coat and unfolding an umbrella as he exited a bath and bawdy house on Papineau.

The bus finally screeched to a halt in front of them, and the folding doors slammed open. As Sayfy gave his daughter his steady hand to step over a patch of black ice and up the step, an Italian woman pushed Salma and barged in front.

"What's the big idea!" Sayfy flicked his hand up in exasperation.

"Go back where you came, maudit syrien!" she belted back.

Sayfy looked to his daughter, who shook her head. She was telling him not to pursue this; there'd be no point. But he'd had just enough nonsense for one day.

"Dit la sale italienne," he snapped. *Says the dirty Italian.*

"Le pape est italien!" she replied. *The Pope is Italian.*

"Les meilleures papes étaient syriens!" *The best popes were Syrian.*

"Bouge-toi!" She pushed Salma again, causing her to cry out.

The tension brewing in Sayfy's chest exploded like a powder keg, and he yanked on the woman's fur overcoat. She stumbled back off the step, slipped on the black ice, and slid under the bus.

The woman screamed and screamed like she was Fay Wray caught in King Kong's mighty grip, and the bus driver just rolled his eyes, shifting into park.

"Papa..." Salma trailed off.

He sighed, adjusted his leather gloves, bent down, grabbed the hysterical nuisance by the collar of her fur coat, and yanked her back onto the sidewalk.

They boarded the bus in silence.

Back at their home on Rue Berri, Sayfy regaled his wife with the details of the incident as Salma went upstairs to chat with Ali.

"Oof," Alzira said, as she set a bowl of soup in front of him at the table. "She was one of those."

"What, Italian?" he asked, taking in a spoonful of the hot, steaming stuff.

"Pious," she replied. "She hates us because we're Orthodox, not Catholic."

"That's not what she said."

"She didn't have to," Alzira began, and Sayfy was sure he was about to get an earful. "These religious denominations were created by people half a gene away from a chimpanzee and it shows."

"Alzira, you have got to learn how to form an opinion."

"Well," she smiled, pausing for effect, "as Gwendolyn remarked in *The Importance of Being Earnest*, sometimes it's not just one's moral duty to speak one's mind, it's also a pleasure."

"No one takes greater pleasure than you," he said, keeping his eyes on his soup, as she went on one of her mouthy tirades. Alzira's tongue would probably lead her straight to hell, but her road there would surely be paved with the bones of people who underestimated her. The fist inside his chest started to clench and tighten its grip again. It took all of Sayfy's wits not to drown face down in his soup bowl, but he finished the last morsel of carrot and potato broth while Alzira yipped like a rabid dog, and then excused himself to his study.

"Oh, Shaf! A package arrived for you earlier!" she called after him. "It's in the rolltop desk!"

Closing the study door behind him, he already knew what he would find once he snipped the twine and unwrapped the brown paper.

Turning down the lamp and drawing the drapes, he quietly flipped his suspenders off his shoulders and slid off his trousers. Next came the collared shirt, giving the pearls their first breath of air all day. Undershirt, socks, and sock garters lay folded neatly atop his desk, as he glanced at himself in the wall mirror, the gingham dress bouncing and twirling about his knobby knees with every turn.

The clenched fist in his chest began to loosen, and he felt his body floating gently.

An idea came to him. In the rolltop desk was the Kodak Retina he had purchased last year for Ali, who quickly abandoned the hobby of photography.

Looking at himself, draped in a beautiful feminine form, complemented by ruby-red gloves and nylons so delicate a fingernail could run them to shreds, he knew he had to zoom in with the lens, focusing solely on his body reflected in the mirror.

If Madame Dineen was to be believed, and the choice was between photographing solely his face or his fashion, he knew which one to choose.

ORTONA

1943

THE HOTEL IN PESCARA was fortified, crenelated, but still open for business. War had been good to them, the bellhop had said as he showed her to her room. Everyone from international reporters like the BBC to ruling magistrates and even high-ranking officials had made good use of the hotel. Naturally, resources were scarce, and they had no restaurant services to offer anymore, but this being Italy, the libations were plentiful. Edna drank like a fish.

When the order came in that night, a Friday, the job was simple. She was to go to an address in Ortona, the western coastal town in Abruzzo where the Canadians were planning on sieging in the coming days. They had to take back control of the town from the fascists, mouse-holing their way through homes to avoid Bavarian snipers, and baptize the entire village by fire. And she needed to gather intel from the Generalleutnant's headquarters before the city was engulfed and destroyed.

The estate is impenetrable, her captain instructed in the orders that were smuggled to her via messenger, written on fine cigarette papers that Nazi checkpoints had failed to inspect. *You are to gather and report any names, contacts, documents found on the Generalleutnant's desk on the lower level. You are to do this on Saturday. We attack at dawn, Sunday.*

She staked out the location. It was the quietest neighbourhood that you could imagine during a time of war. On a thoroughfare lined with huge estates and beautiful gardens, there wasn't so much as a dog barking, a car moving, or a stable horse whinnying. *A ghost neighbourhood,* Edna thought. The original owners were probably on transports to far Eastern Europe by now, she figured. Everyone had heard the stories coming out of Poland, Yugoslavia, and the borderlands with the Soviets. These were the kind of homes the fascists loved to commandeer as command posts.

Her target building, a villa-style mansion with a massive set of stone steps up the front, reminded her of the Oratoire St-Joseph in Montreal. Catholic pilgrims would climb up to the cathedral on their knees, and so she figured when she broke in she would do the same.

The grounds were oddly quiet. Not a light or a body stirred in what was supposed to be the Nazi base for operations in this region. The roof was terracotta and the exterior had grape vines crawling up to the sky.

There's no one in the street, never mind the house, she thought. She peered through the wrought-iron gate to the entryway steps, touching the metal, and it moved slightly. It wasn't even locked.

So she hitched a ride back to the hotel in Pescara with a coal porter on horseback to prepare for her mission.

At nine o'clock, Edna ran a bath. As the hotel porters ran in and out with buckets of partly boiled water from the well, she poured a couple of drinks, thinking she'd have an early night to be ready to go the next evening.

But as the cast-iron tub filled before her, she had another thought. She shooed the porters away.

Changing into her trekking clothes, she reasoned, *It's empty. It's easy. This'll be over so quickly the bathwater'll still be hot when I get back.* Yes, her commander had specifically instructed Edna to go Saturday night, not the hours before Saturday dawn, but what was the point of waiting?

She grabbed the hotel bottle opener from the vanity drawer in case she needed to improvise and set out to do the job.

There was a spot near the ruins of the cathedral spire where the British had buried rations. Edna unearthed dry goods: sugar, saltines, tea bags, and cocoa. They would come in handy on the road. She stuffed them into a yellow linen sack next to the bottle opener, her only belonging. She knew to never carry anything she didn't need. Always travel as light as you can.

The morning had not broken yet. The burning stars above moved like the moon over waves. The leaves whispered and the branches hissed. The British had given her a pair of boots, size forty-two, much too big, but boots all the same. She had also procured a pair of itchy woollen black pants and a striped mariner shirt. Both were too large for her frame, but a discarded safety pin she'd found in the vanity table at the hotel enabled her to fasten them together snugly.

As she left Pescara behind, she marvelled at how quickly it disappeared from view. The mountainous path near the shoreline swallowed the city up, and there was nothing more to be heard. The rock break walls kept secrets well. Any gunshots, wails, or moans of war were staunched and swiftly cauterized.

As Edna walked among the ruins of the countryside, she thought of her last day in Montreal.

"You can pass for anything," her superiors had said when they enlisted her. She spoke French, Italian, German, and Arabic. In school, she had taken to track and field and even won a few races. Her dark hair contrasted with her pale skin. That made her an excellent tool. A tool for reconnaissance.

That same night, in the last days of the 1930s, she had

found herself on a transport to Portsmouth, and she had been put to work ever since. She was in Brussels when it capitulated. In Paris the night before the armies of darkness marched under l'Arc de triomphe. She gathered information, slipping in and out of estates, ballrooms, and bunkers like a northwestern breeze.

Now, her cheeks were a milky cream, almost luminous in the moonlight. She reached down to the muddy path, grabbed a glop of dirt, and rubbed it into her face. Any lights would reflect off her skin, giving her away immediately.

"You will be the death of me," she whispered to herself, thinking of her skin but also of the Canadian army that had sent her here.

There had been a Luftwaffe air raid in Ortona the night before. She'd heard distant booms and shudders that made the hotel walls pop and floorboards bubble. Now, the ruined farms on the outskirts of town were silent. All the cows, pigs, and livestock had either been stolen by bandits or slaughtered in the air raids. As she walked, she ignored the jittering bricks and unsound foundations around her. When a house collapsed a mere fifty metres in front of her, she was swallowed by the fumes and suspended debris. Finding her footing, she carried on, knees bloody and face black like a miner's.

She had lost all sense of fear long ago. After the first time she'd bedded a comando di brigata to steal top-secret cables with orders from Il Duce, she emerged world-weary and battle tested. She'd done hundreds of jobs and felt like an old lady at the age of twenty. Nothing shocked her now. Her own walls were thicker than solid rock.

It was closing in on 4:00 a.m., the quietest time of night. Before the larks and roosters called. Before the Abruzzo farmers and townsfolk harvested their plums and olives. Before the Nazi commandants woke up, still at the brothels, pants around their ankles, and rushed to dress.

As Edna closed in on the target house once more in a single night, she thought of the Obergruppenführer she'd bedded the summer prior in Prague. He had tiny eyes the colour of French Chartreuse, and his cheeks were flushed with salmon-toned blotches. He wore a suit and his ears looked like chanterelles. He spoke of his wife and children the entire time as he spread her thighs and slammed his body into hers until she thought she might split. She felt her neck stained by his grip that almost strangled her, but she pointed her heels to Jesus, thinking of all the women in her family who had endured worse. Sex is easier to clean up than war.

As he lay passed out, she pocketed an iron key from his key ring. A copy of that key was later used to break Slovak dissidents out of Pankrác Prison. She escaped on foot through the forests of Bohemia and Moravia, and then was smuggled into Yugoslavia, where she was shipped by sea transport into Italy. By the end of the year, the

Obergruppenführer had been assassinated on the streets of Prague by both Czech and Slovak patriots, and Edna had been treated for a venereal disease and pregnancy.

The Allied doctor charged with her care remarked when he thought she was under anesthesia that he'd never heard of an Arab woman under the employ of Canada's armed forces before.

"At least this termination will prevent more Mohammedans from flooding the world," he said.

It was not lost on her that the Nazi Generalleutnant had a name uncannily similar to that of the Obergruppenführer, whom the Czechs had dubbed the "Butcher of Prague." Their family names were the same but for a small aberration in spelling. Their given names were almost identical. *Nazis are all the same*, she mused.

She stayed clear of the railway tracks and tunnels that cut through the hills. Intelligence told her the Jerries slept in the tunnels during the air raids. Once she passed the village of Tollo, she ducked away from the coastline to get up the ridge. She steadied herself as the villa came into view near the ancient Ortona castle, crumbling from the raids. All her food was still uneaten in her pack. She tucked it behind the trunk of an olive tree: a treat for later. But she took the bottle opener from the sack and shoved it into her sock.

She pushed through the wrought-iron gate, still unlocked. A telephone rang from inside the estate. At the bottom of the long colonnade stairway entrance, Edna paused. Her instinct was to duck into the bushes, but something stopped her. The telephone rang and rang. Five, seven, ten times. Nobody was there to answer it.

"This is gonna be easy." She repeated her thought aloud like a comfort. She crept around the garden retaining wall that led to the back and crawled on her knees up the rear steps to a set of French doors. Grabbing the bottle opener to jimmy the lock, she smirked at the inane decision to install French doors over these impossible English oak doors. Security only works if you use it, and if all her jobs had taught her anything, it was that anyone with French doors just isn't serious.

As she held the bottle opener to the handle, she thought of the open front gate. *Just try first*, she thought. She put the bottle opener down on the ground, covered it with a few leaves, and grabbed the door handle.

With a *fump* and a *screeee*, the door opened.

This guy's headquarters are impenetrable? Edna scoffed, recalling her orders. *What a load of hogwash. He doesn't even bother to lock his doors.*

And in she went. After her eyes adjusted to the dark, she took stock that the rear room was clearly once a bedroom, still sporting an unmade bed, probably belonging to an Generale d'Armata before Italy capitulated to the Allies and the Nazis invaded Italy earlier that year. Most Italian generals, high-ranking officials, and dignitaries were smuggled out through Sicily before the battles began. In peacetime, Ortona had a large population, but as Edna passed oil portraits on the wall, each featuring an olive-skinned beauty with thick curly hair and ruby lips, she knew she was looking at ghosts.

Pushing farther into the compound, she left the bedroom behind, hugging the walls, and found herself at the top of a landing, leading down a curved stairwell to the lower level. Using the glow of the moon as her only light source, she descended, and, sure enough, exactly as she had been instructed, she found herself in an office with a curious fish-bowl sitting on the desk. There were no fish, but the water was fresh. Not a speck of dust or film to be found atop the surface. The place was empty but not abandoned, she reasoned.

The office smelled of sandalwood, and a leather throne of a chair sat before the desk. *This is lovely*, she thought, taking a seat. *Very unlived-in but fine.* To her delight, she found the chair had a swivel base, just like the ones under the men at the Bank of Montreal who brokered her father's mortgage. She did a little spin, using the fishbowl as a reference point.

She hadn't thought about her father in a long time. When his business affairs went bad, he tried to pawn her off on her aunt, but Aunty Salma refused to take her in, so she became a ward. That's how the Department of National Defence found her at sixteen. A scout noticed her at a jazz club trying to make it past the doorman. When the doorman insisted her name wasn't on the list, she accidentally-on-purpose knocked the hat-check girl's martini out of her hands, splashing it all over his pants.

"Oh, dear heavens! I do apologize, sir! How clumsy of me!" she exclaimed, reaching down to his crotch to wipe away the booze. He flinched and grabbed her hands in horror that she might molest his manhood.

A crowd gathered to giggle, and the doorman waved her inside just to put a swift end to the scene. At the bar, a man in a hat bought her a drink. "Have you ever thought about applying those skills of yours to serve king and country?" he asked.

"If you're asking to spend the night with me, I must give you top marks for originality," she quipped.

Wards made excellent recruits, she came to learn, because they had no ties and nothing to live for. Plus, the minister of national defence depended on agents who had no trouble using their carnal knowledge. Sex had most likely already been devalued for a ward at a young age, so if they must bed a target or a mole, it was just another five minutes out of their day.

"What's your name?" the agent asked, as he passed her his business card. She noticed there was no name on it, just an address and a time to meet the following day.

"Edna," she lied. And that's how she was known ever since. Perhaps she would have been considered unpatriotic with an Arabic name. But thinking of her family, who fled Lebanon because they were being persecuted by the Druze, she did wonder if, when she joined them in heaven, they would recognize her. When they called out her real name, would she even know to answer?

Edna stopped spinning in the office chair and looked at the empty fishbowl for a long time. She suddenly had the urge to smash it against the wall.

Steadying herself against the desk, she began digging through documents. Folders and papers, address books and telegrams were strewn about. Most of it was rubbish; the Nazis sent telegrams for everything, including weekly meteorological forecasts and dress code violations. But it wasn't long before she found cables concerning the Luftwaffe and paratrooper plans for the following day. Numbers of men on foot and numbers of reserves. The strength of their ranks and orders to hold the bridge at all costs, even should they receive no cover from the Luftwaffe. Names of high-ranking Canadian officials that should be targeted. Details on the make and composite of Royal Canadian Air Force planes like the Hawkers and the de Havillands. There were also names of Italians known to be dissidents who should be reported to the Gestapo. Hotels that should be searched and seized. Pogroms to instigate.

Farms to burn. Streets to booby-trap with land mines for any retreating enemies. She saw the name of her own hotel on the list, with orders to shoot all staff suspected of aiding enemy forces.

Then she saw two sets of headlights pull up outside the house.

The office was on the ground floor with windows all around, and the headlights illuminated the hall just beyond the desk. Edna grabbed the documents she was to take and dashed out of the office, toppling the swivel chair onto the carpet. In the front drive, two large malachite Kübelwagens came to a halt on the gravel, and two heavies in boots jumped out of each vehicle.

What kind of person doesn't bother locking his doors? The type of person who wouldn't worry should someone break in.

Edna ran back up the stairs, through the rear bedroom, and out the French doors. She got halfway down the exterior rear stairs when she tripped, taking the rest at a tumble. The noise of her body hitting the stones changed the direction of the boots out front, and she could tell they were seconds away.

To her left was the wall of the garden, so she flung herself into it, thorns and nettles be damned. Given that light was slowly breaking over the horizon, the bush would hide her shadow on top of concealing her body. She took a deep breath and shoved her face down into the December mud, knowing full well that her skin would reflect light and show up against the darkness, the soil, and her clothes.

If they find me... her brain screamed as her heartbeat throbbed against the branches of the garden bushes. She was certain each palpitation was shaking the boughs obscenely.

As the boots rounded the side of the estate, crunching on the gravel path, and the heavies ascended the rear stairs, she knew that this was not something she could get out of. The heavies looked like they had absolutely no sense of humour whatsoever. She couldn't smile her way out of it. She couldn't fuck her way out of it.

They entered the estate, and it was obvious all at once that they were there to look for her. They kept going in and out, speaking in hushed German, so she could only make out a few words. Töte sie. *Kill her.* She heard them pulling out their guns and cocking them.

I've used up my nine lives, she thought, paralyzed. She knew it would be the wrong choice to get up and run with them so close.

If anything happens now, no one knows who or where I am. Not the department, not the hotel, not a single person in Montreal, she realized.

For a brief moment, she allowed herself to indulge in the fantasy of an international manhunt, or even newspaper headlines. "CANADIAN WOMAN GOES MISSING ON ITAL-IAN FRONT." "BUSINESSWOMAN NEVER FOUND." That was her cover. But no one even knew her name.

She came a day early, so even her captain wasn't aware of her location. It wouldn't be in his or Canada's best interest to announce her disappearance. In fact, they would disavow her and any culpability. She was alone.

And then, just as quickly as they turned up, the heavies ran out of the house, slammed the door, got into their four-by-fours, and left.

Edna waited ten minutes, face down in the mud, before she wobbled to her feet. Her hair was full of twigs, her face cut with tiny lacerations, and she was covered in gunk. The documents, too, were dripping in her hand. She fisted them.

Her brain was screaming at her to run, but you never run. So she pushed out of the gate and began the long walk back to Pescara. Once she was down the ridge and past the trees with olives too sour to eat from the vine, she gradually picked up speed and did run in the end, but not for a long time.

When she reached a vineyard just outside of Pescara, about five kilometres from the hotel, she rang the bell and asked the vintner if she might use his telephone.

Ringing her contact in Sicily, she whispered, "Go secure."

"Code."

"Echo Tango 4-7."

"Go ahead."

"Jerry ran in. I couldn't get anything."

He paused for the length of a Bible. "You were supposed to go in on Saturday."

"I barely got away with my life."

"And how many lives will be lost because you jumped the gun?"

There was a click on the line. She was dismissed.

The vintner, an old Italian nonno in a tweed cap, came in with a wet towel so she could wipe the muck off her face. The sight of her must have been something else, like she had just wandered out of a POW camp.

"Bevanda?" he asked.

"Something very alcoholic but a kid could drink," she replied in Italian, remembering her training. *You need sugar when your adrenalin kicks off,* they had drilled into her.

The nonno raised an eyebrow. "Tough night?"

She nodded as she wiped down her cheeks. But as soon as the nonno returned with a bottle of something from his cellar and a corkscrew, she bolted to her feet and ran out the door.

The bottle opener, she realized. She had left it at the scene. And the bag of rations she had left behind the tree—they were inside British army standard ration tins.

As the sun rose, she approached the hotel. The place

was deserted. Valises and papers were strewn about the floor, shoes and overcoats tossed to the side. Not a bell-hop at the door, not a concierge behind the desk fortified with sandbags. Taken God knows where. Transported like cattle. Standing in a shallow hole. The forest swallowing any sounds of rifle fire. And it was because of her.

Edna went to her room. The bathwater, sitting undisturbed in the tub, was cold.

That night, the opposing armies would gather at their front lines. And the next day, the infamous bloody Battle of Ortona would rage, killing hundreds of Canadian soldiers in brutal hand-to-hand combat. Bodies exploded into pink mists, while cathedrals toppled in grey ones. Those who survived walked away with hastily patched-up bodies. Limbs missing. Faces stained with horror.

And a dark-haired woman no one had ever laid eyes on before would be found a week later by the victorious Canadian forces of the Loyal Edmonton Regiment. They would keep her discovery a secret. No bulletins went out over the wireless; no international headlines decried her disappearance. The official report, classified by the minister of national defence, simply stated that she was "submerged in a freezing cold bathtub, her wrists slit, and a sign hung from her neck that read, *My name is Fadwa*."

MONTREAL AWAITS YOU

1949

April 23, 1949

My Dearest Nasir,

You may have heard my long-suffering husband, Shafeek, passed last winter. He died as he lived: surrounded by those who loved him, and wearing my garter belt under his clothing. At the mercy meal after the funeral, my daughter, Salma, reminded me that I had often spoken of you. Despite her grief, she had the audacity to suggest I reach out to you and request the pleasure of your presence. So here I am. Don't spend another minute thinking about it. Montreal awaits you.

The French may have stolen our dear Beirut, but they have been driven out of Montreal. They are all Canadians now, and the tongue is different. They are constantly talking about tabernacles and chalices. Catholics, don't ya know! I wish my French were better to get the nuance of the slang, but for everyday purposes, it suits me just fine.

Book your passage and come today. This summer, at the latest. Because Montreal changes from year to year, and it may not be as it is now by next year.

Every person you meet on the Main looks like they either just starred in a Clark Gable movie, or they turned down a part in a Clark Gable movie. In either case, there are plenty of charmers and knockouts. My second-floor walk-up on Drolet overlooks Mont-Royal, where every night there are street musicians and clowns busking for attention. In the morning, the scent of steamés fills the air, and you can buy five hot dogs for twenty-five cents. Once, I found a quarter on the street. That day, the Zakaib sisters, Mademoiselle Ayoub who lives below me, and I ate like queens. We're still on rations, but if you make friends with Atwater grocers, they will let you nibble on a handful of cherries or cut you a cantaloupe slice without even entertaining the thought of payment.

Montreal is alive with colour. Neon signs light up Sainte-Catherine's, and the movies at the Empress Theatre are first run and funny. I would take you there—should you hurry up—for a nickel! If you ask nicely, I'll treat you to popcorn as well (if you move your caboose). And if you play your cards right, the night needn't end there. That's if you're interested in playing cards. I was never one for poker or rummy, but my deck is stacked.

Tourists sit at marble-topped tables peppering the cafés

that are lined up like soldiers along Saint-Denis. Window displays of ladies' hosiery, umbrellas, silk ties, and the most frivolous chapeaux stretch as far as the eye can see. There's always work for a seamstress like me, and it's enough to keep me in meats and malts, but I'm no Rockefeller. So I window shop, which is a Montrealer Olympic sport. I wear all these different pairs of shoes during the spring. Each one hurts my feet in a different way. I'm nurturing these calluses, trying to build up scars. I'm waiting for it to hurt, then heal, then hurt again. I am building these walls for a reason. I know these sandals will cut right across the top of my foot, so I douse my feet, which are covered in lacerations, in talcum powder before I set out for the day. Yet I would never go barefoot. I would never think of it. Shoes are appealing for a reason. When the wind blows my dress up for a moment, I can see them better. And so could you, were you to walk these narrow, charming thoroughfares by my side.

Montreal sits on the slope of a hilltop, and everyone walks on a slant as they move from Viger up Saint-Hubert to the Plateau. Fiacres will take you up the mount to the Belvedere lookout for sixty cents, if you've got that to spare, and the view is well worth it. Looking down upon the Saint Lawrence, it's easy to imagine the waters that flow under the Cartier Bridge once ebbed from the shores of Beirut. We all come from somewhere—why shouldn't the current?

The birds on Île-Sainte-Hélène sing the same songs as the ones on the foothills of Rashaya al-Wadi. I promise you will know the lyrics off by heart. We sang those songs together once, underneath a cedar tree.

When I saw you last, before I set off from Beirut's port to Canada, you told me the pain of separation wouldn't be much. You'd follow soon, you promised. I removed my white glove then, and when no one was looking, you reached out and ran your fingers over mine, lingering on the smallest. Had my mother or my sito seen that, they would have smacked me on the nose. But we were always rather good at private moments in public. More moments like that were sure to follow.

Then that hullabaloo in Europe broke out. The Allied blockade meant food and fuel prices were too much, I understand. Letters became a frivolity when there were more pressing matters at hand. Winters in Montreal leave everyone bundled and burdened. Heaps of snow higher than two metres will make you a housebound prisoner unless you like to toboggan out of the second-floor window. So perhaps you think me mad to write to you now, after all this time of separation and silence, and after so much has transpired.

It's not for nothing I didn't write, mind you. I heard you married Saïdé. I can't hold that against you, even though I want to. I should make you repent or beg for mercy, especially since I know what's good for you. But she was a dear friend and no doubt a doting and pious wife. I was as besotted with her as you must have been. Of course, she and I knew each other since infancy. Perhaps you knew this, but as a child, she looked rather haggard, like something that would eat its young. But what a beauty she became. I'm not jealous (maybe a little). No, not one bit (okay, a bit).

All of that animosity we can leave behind now because the views in Montreal will make you recall the Bekaa Valley, and the Lachine Canal is so much like La Corniche. Let us walk up the grand stairs of Oratoire St-Joseph on our knees. Let us buy haunches of pork from the Marché Jean Talon and feast like sultans. Let's sit at the long, hot lunch counter at Beauty's and drink strawberry milkshakes until they kick us out for giggling and depravity. I want to do all of that with you. And Montreal is the place to do it.

I have found a nice pied-à-terre for you on Rue Berri, near the train tracks on Rosemont. You can pay forty-five cents a day for room and board, and we can ride bicyclettes up to Parc Jarry and back. You just have to promise to come.

I am truly mad about the Montreal people and everything to do with this town. At Druxy's around the corner they make the best mustard spread and jarred spiced jams, and they exclaim, "Bienvenue, habibti," every time they see me coming. Jews from Europe and Arabs exiled from the

Nakba mingle like close cousins here. I would miss them all so much were I ever to leave. But truth be told, I miss other people even more. My people. People I once knew and even the familiar faces of people who look like me. Sure, I've got the Ayoubs, Zakaibs, and Khourys to keep me good company, but so many of the people I miss, my people, are gone. My children, Salma and Ali, have moved on to greener pastures—she got married, and he preceded his father to the unknown. Ali got away from us a bit at the end of the 1930s. The wrong people always lead to the wrong choices. He even had a daughter, but we've never had the displeasure of her company, or even meeting her mother. I've suffered great losses in recent years, my old friend. Great losses, indeed.

Now, with the summer coming, I don't want to be so far away from my people anymore. I can make you powdered eggs and coffee with clotted cream for breakfast and read you some poetry that I procured from an estate sale in Côte-des-Neiges. These poets are worth their weight in booze and butter. "Miniver Cheevy born too late. Miniver coughed and called it fate."

An edge of spring is in the air. The sky is crimson in the east, a pale blue-grey above, with hazy strokes of purple and grizzly clouds that blend into each other like water paints. Mademoiselle Ayoub's bulbs finally blossomed, and they are the colour of cream. They remind me of a young man

I once knew many years ago. The man with the pollinated eyes. His face, a warm flower. I don't mind saying that I've gotten on in years, though I can't understand how I got to be old all of a sudden. Wasn't it just yesterday that we lay together in the grass over the hill from your father's goat farm and watched the clouds take the shape of our bodies? One of the old Jewish butchers at Druxy's told me his age the other day after slicing my half pound of smoked meat: sixty-six. He doesn't look it. Well, if I'm being honest (and you always preferred me that way), Montreal makes young 'uns of us all. After all, should you come here—and you really should—we can feel sixteen again.

Please find enclosed four recent photographs I took at the photomaton in Bonaventure station yesterday. If they don't find their way into your hands, I hope they will find their way to your children.

I hope you don't think I've become a fallen woman in all this time. Perhaps I am being forward, but I think Montreal wants us both to be on her island shores. She wants us both inside her. A few years ago, I saw a delightfully scandalous Mae West movie (as all her pictures are, and I love her for them). She said something that stuck with me long after I walked out of the cinema, though the movie plot entirely escapes me. She cooed, "You only live once, but if you do it right, once is enough." Dear Nasir, isn't that just about everything?

Then again, she also once said, "It's not the men in your life that counts; it's the life in your men!"

I'm not sure precisely where to send this letter; I have a box of these addressed to you in the hall. Perhaps this will be the one that makes it.

The inquiries on behalf of the church say that you and Saïdé have been missing since the cessation of arms, but I don't believe it. The priest seems to be very sure of himself, but he's a crook and a liar. Preaching about women's obedience in a marriage rather than praising women's contributions! The fairer sex is the backbone of society, but he wants men to be the boss? Like Sito always said, beauty is skin deep, but ugly goes clean to the bone. And if heaven is full of louts like him, then hand me the sunscreen for hell. The Syrian ladies have their own benevolent society here, where we humour him but do what we want. Sometimes when he visits our meetings, we slip some laudanum into his coffee. Once he's snoring away, we discuss our favourite passages of *Lady Chatterley's Lover*. He wakes to find us busy with embroidery and goes home to his wife, patting himself on the back. He's not very bright, and I must say, I admire that in a man. Present company excluded, of course.

Even if you don't reply, I do hope this letter finds you, and finds you well. And if you've had enough of this trial separation, perhaps you will come. The Montreal people are crazy, but I'm in love with their craziness.

And I'm in love with you, Nasir. I was back then, and I still am today. I remember you as the most handsome man in Rashaya. Which you were. Which you will forever be.

Just know that in life, you can always start again. With a new love or, in this case, an old one. In a new city or country. Pick up a new instrument. Change your signature. Walk with a bit less (or a bit more) bounce. Take the opposite opinion to all your friends.

And if that's what you choose, then, my dear Nasir, Montreal is the place for you.

With hope and love (and all the disasters therein),
Your Alzira

~

July 30, 1949

So there you are, dear Alzira!

Now I promise to write at length. It's strange how much happiness you feel when people reappear, especially those to whom you have felt bound since youth. You realize that you have never lost each other fully. I was saddened to read of your curious husband's passing. We all have had some experience with the French after they stole our country, so you will know all the regular whisperings about their libertine ways, but are the French Canadians another breed? You shall have to fill me in on Shafeek's, shall we say, proclivities.

I was allowed to have a rich, fulfilled life, even if it was full of conflict. The Allied invasion of Vichy French Lebanon brought many hardships to our family, including the loss of people who were very dear to me. But what did that matter when I lost you so many years before?

By some mercy of God, our street did not see much action and our family home in Rashaya still stands. Nevertheless, I was forced into exile in Palestine—a journey that still haunts me to this day. Then the Nakba forced me out of Palestine, under gruesome circumstances, which I am afraid to put to paper, should this letter be opened by the censors. Later, I started a distance-learning degree and worked, until recently, in the fields of art and literature. I "live" in a one-room Cairo flat, with a shared lavatory down the hall. After circumventing the postal systems of these broken countries, your letter finally found its way here. Outside my window that overlooks the busy market street, I hear the loud voices of tourists haggling for souvenir prayer rugs or thimbles or saffron to bring home. I always lean over the railing, peering down, hoping one of those tourists bears a resemblance to you.

It's not a bad life, really. The neighbourhood sharmootas from the brothel next door entertain me each morning over coffee with their stories of how ungallant the British forces are with their trousers down. That keeps me endlessly amused.

Exile suits me. I have entered a new peace of mind; it's what I've always longed for. I used to have dreams of being the next Robinson Crusoe: to see the sun rise in Southern India, to live among the Bedouin, to hear the call of the lions over the Serengeti, and, yes, to speak Québécois French (poorly) with a girl I once loved. Now, I just want to feel my feet walk on the earth. I want to look for my lost family among the green and natural things that are left. I want to see the ice before it melts.

Yes, Saïdé and I did wed. God forgive me, I did love her. But I couldn't even mourn her in the terrible aftermath of the Battle of Sidon in 1941. That's what the Australians called the town. Didn't they know it was her town? As you know, it was named after her almost precisely: Saida! She disappeared, along with several other women. Some bodies were later found washed up on the shores of Tyre, with obvious signs of brutalization. Her body never resurfaced. My children came with me to Palestine, but after the Nakba, they decided to resettle in Nablus. How strange that once they come of age, children have the audacity to determine their own destiny. How strange that it only seemed natural to us as well at that age. N'est-ce pas?

Of course I still remember the songs we sang under the cedar trees. Do you still sing of that orange-filled dusk when the leaves were the same colour as your eyes?

Regretfully, I rarely find time for music anymore. And my home organ I had to give away. I enjoy remembering how the two of us played for each other (Alfred Moffat—I think I still have the sheet music) back then at my mother's. It must have been 1900. Remember the books we exchanged, like exiled poet Nazim Hikmet? Remember gawking at obscene postcards that were passed illicitly through the student body from hand to hand? Your typewritten poems I also still have. I still remember how you, embarrassed, put them in my hand, shortly before you sailed away.

Objects have the longest memories of all; beneath their stillness, they are alive with the terrors they have witnessed. I smuggled your poems out of Palestine by filling them with tobacco and wrapping them in cigarette papers. The patrolling squads didn't so much as glance at them. Every time the urge struck, I had to remind myself not to smoke. Upon receiving your letter this week, I unravelled the poems from their hiding spot. Tightly wound all these years, and yellowed by the tobacco, the words shook me less than the sight of the foolscap in my hands. Somewhere in there were your fingerprints. It was almost like holding your hand again, ever so briefly, at the port that day we said goodbye. Sometimes I wish I had left with you that day.

Yes, I do want to join you in Montreal, because everything that is divine in this earth is telling me that I will find what I am looking for there. I can hear the voices lost in the war there. Let us make these plans immediately and without delay.

But, Alzira, you know what they say. If you want to make God laugh, tell him you have a plan. Things being the way they are, I cannot find my way forward to you. I've had far too much trouble, enough for a lifetime. How could I ever even make it past a single checkpoint or border crossing? To say nothing of traversing the Mediterranean, let alone an entire ocean. Montreal is a lifetime and three decades ago. I lost it from my sights the moment your steamship disappeared from the Beirut horizon. Things change. And, not for nothing, I have changed.

I am old, set in my ways, endlessly stubborn, ornery, and taciturn. I stink, I smoke, I swear up a terrible storm when I'm drunk, and I only eat rubbish. My wounds define me, and now I have nothing but my scars. They forge a powerful path upon my skin. The map of my life is written in my scars. And they do not point westward.

Should you ever find yourself making the journey back east, please do write. I'll expect you, and I'll find an organ worthy of Moffat.

Many good wishes for you and your family. Give greetings to your blessed daughter. And to the city of Montreal, fascinating as she sounds.

In heartfelt solidarity,

The man you once knew

THE BELLY DANCER

1971

I WAS SITTING IN the living room with my parents, watching *The Ed Sullivan Show*. Nancy Sinatra was wearing a pink minidress and reclining on the stage. Her bouffant blond hair swept over her forehead as she crooned a slow song.

The telephone in the kitchen rang. There were three types of phone calls: 1. Wrong number; 2. Sito calling just to yack; and 3. Bad news. I could tell it was the third one, even before I picked up the receiver.

"Naseema, it's me."

"Gustave, what's the matter?"

"I'm so sorry," he said. "I'm so very sorry."

I peered round the bend to the living room to see if my parents' ears had perked. They had not. I picked up the rotary base and moved farther behind the kitchen wall toward the sink, the curly cord stretching to its limit.

I whispered, "What happened?"

"It's Manitoba," he began. "It's been messing with me ever since I arrived last month. The weather, the people. It's testing me."

"Testing you how?" I cupped my mouth so my voice wouldn't bounce off the glass-fronted cabinets and skillets hanging behind the convection oven.

"Maybe our engagement happened too fast, maybe we should have waited until my reassignment was done, I don't know," he rambled, and I could hear the distant hum of a jukebox and the clacking of cutlery.

"Where are you?" I asked.

"In the telephone box at the Rusty Anchor."

"You're drunk."

"No, Naseema, you don't understand. I'm thinking clearly for the first time in months. And what I think is . . ." As he spoke, his words seemed to garble, and all I could hear was the echo from the living room television set. Nancy made the sound of a pistol firing, singing that her love had shot her down.

"I'm coming to Portage la Prairie." I suddenly raised my voice.

Ma's voice piped up from the other room. "Naseema, who's on the phone?"

"You're coming here?" I could hear the surprise in Gustave's voice over the line. "Okay, that's good. Yes, come, and we can talk."

Nancy's voice whispered mournfully into the microphone. Her lover had shot her down.

AS MY PLANE took off from Dorval, my mind was swirling with questions. This flight would be counted by seconds, not minutes or hours. I decided to spend the first 1,800 seconds going over what I might have missed in our early courtship.

I met Gustave in the McGill library last year. The chesterfields in the common areas faced each other, and while I read my textbooks detailing Constantine's founding of the Byzantine Empire, across from me napped a blond Québécois man with a chiseled jawline like George Peppard's. I ripped out a page from my notebook and began to draw him. During the FLQ crisis around that time, my roommate and I defied curfew to go downtown and flirt with the soldiers posted at checkpoints near every intersection. She came up with the brilliant idea of hastily drawing their portraits, and then handing them to the men in uniform, our dormitory telephone number conveniently pencilled in at the bottom next to our names.

When Gustave finally roused, his textbook still open on his chest, our eyes met and he smiled. I don't know how I did this—I could never do this again—but I leaned over to hand him the drawing with a smile and told him my name. He looked at my sketch of his face—eyes closed, brows furrowed, cheek smushed into the armrest—and it took him a minute to realize it was him. We talked for two hours on those green chesterfields.

Ma was not exactly pleased about my choice of boyfriend. Dating a white Québécois man was grounds for disowning. I'd long heard about the troubles she'd experienced growing up in Little Italy. Granted, she and Daddy were already upset that I had decided to move out of their house before I was married and live in the university dorms. Polite girls just didn't do that. Three years ago, my father forbade me from attending the Beatles concert at the Montreal Forum after I won tickets off the radio.

"No daughter of mine is going to a rock concert," he had said. "Only loose girls who do drugs do that." For me, that was the last straw.

I still visited them in Ville Saint-Laurent for Saturday night dinner, where Sito would mumble something about her only granddaughter deserving to have Tabasco sauce poured down her throat. She'd then swear, "Q'iss imick," but Ma always told Sito to hush up. "Q'iss imik" means "your mother's cunt." Not something to bring up at my mother's dinner table.

Sometimes I'd answer the dormitory telephone to hear, "Is this Naseema?"

"Yes, Ma, it's me."

She'd then sob for five minutes before hanging up.

I spent the next 7,200 seconds poking holes in our engagement as I flew over Ontario. I'm not one for grand gestures, and Gustave knew that. No dropping to one knee or making a big song and dance about it. We were having coffee on Sainte-Catherine's and he suggested it might be a good idea if we got married. Later that week, I went with him to the jeweller's on University Avenue and picked out my own ring. He didn't ask Daddy's permission first, which didn't help matters, so we had a Saturday night dinner together at their place on Rue Dépatie.

I was nervous, and maybe Gustave was as well. Nerves can make people act in the strangest ways. Because it all stopped before it even began as we sat at the table. Ma did what she always does, which is lay out small dishes of sliced cucumber and tomato, some black olives, and some homemade laban. Gustave asked for some white bread, so I got up and cut some Syrian flatbread into triangles and placed them in front of him.

Under his breath, he muttered, "I said white."

Daddy looked down the rims of his spectacles from the head of the table, and Ma froze. I quickly moved to Gustave's side and got down on my knees to ask him what the matter was.

"Get up off your knees!" Ma snapped, and I jumped.

"Ma, I was just—"

"You don't beg on your knees for any man!"

Daddy folded his arms and smirked at Gustave. "Welcome to the NFL."

Gustave and I hadn't made love yet, though I told him I wanted to. My family had long stamped out the practice of checking the bedsheets on the first night of a union, I assured him. He told me he'd always dreamed of having a virgin wife who was his and his alone, and I wanted him to have that. So I moved back from the dorms to Rue Dépatie.

At our engagement party, I belly danced, just like my aunties had taught me. Ma and daddy's cousins, my sitos on both sides, and even my jido on Daddy's side came to the legion hall in Ville Saint-Laurent for the occasion. Gustave's family was very polite. They weren't sure about a lot of the Lebanese food laid out at the buffet, but they nibbled unobtrusively and drank a lot of Daddy's prepaid bar tab.

Everyone turned their chairs outward from their tables as I took to the parquet dance floor in my green bejewelled halter and puffy pantaloons, the coin belt jangling around my hips. The man in the disc jockey booth played "Ya Habibi Dawabni Al-Hawa," and Cousin Dawood played the darbuka as I clicked my finger cymbals and swirled my hips toward each seated guest. I gyrated like I was trying to shake off my womanly parts and become an angel. My stomach undulated, and I pointed my painted toes like they were pistols. When I clapped, everyone clapped along. When I arched my back and bent backwards, my arms curving toward Jesus, Gustave stomped his feet. My uncles were three sheets to the wind, so they kept getting up from their chairs to try to dance with me, but my aunties slammed them back down, smacking them upside their heads.

Gustave's parents smiled and clapped but looked away every time I got close. Gustave's sisters whispered to each other, but they clapped along, too. Gustave got up from his chair and threw up in the bathroom.

As I drove us home that night, he apologized for being a lush. "You were beautiful," he slurred over and over again. But before he passed out in the passenger seat, he mumbled how unfortunate it was Premier Lesage had lowered the voting age to eighteen a few years ago because he was hoping to have a wife who "thinks like me."

I spent the final 1,800 seconds of the flight pondering what I loved about Gustave. As my plane made its final descent toward Winnipeg, where I would have to run to catch my propeller plane to Portage la Prairie, I thought about his square jaw, his blond hair that reflected sunshine bouncing off the Lachine Canal, the way he always had this faraway look in his eyes. I wanted my children to look as effortlessly cool as he did, flicking a Pall Mall with a snap of his fingers. I thought about how he squeezed my hand three times as we waited at traffic lights—translating to "I," "Love," and "You."

There was a lot to admire about the man. He came from a good family—one that wouldn't care if their daughter-in-law attended a Beatles concert. He'd studied radio engineering at McGill, and he had an exciting career. I wanted to support him in that career.

In the early stages of our wedding planning, Gustave had received word from his bosses that he was to be transferred to Portage la Prairie to set up their new radio tower. We reasoned that it would only be for a few months. A year, tops. I drove him to Dorval a month ago, a Buffy Sainte-Marie song playing on the car radio, and we hugged and cried at the gate before he boarded his plane.

"You're so loyal," he whispered in my ear. "I'm so glad I chose you."

The loudspeaker shrieked arrivals and gate changes and last calls for boarding above our heads.

"Call me every day," I sniffled.

"Expect one every hour," he promised, and then turned down the walkway toward his awaiting airbus.

On the drive home alone, Leonard Cohen sang a song about goodbyes, and what a shambles we make of them.

As the plane's wheels bounced and scratched the tarmac, I gripped the armrests, trying to shake the thought that maybe Gustave didn't choose me. Maybe I chose him. And maybe I knew why.

~

I TOOK A TAXI from the Portage la Prairie airfield to my hotel, where the front desk clerk handed me a telegram.

WILL CALL ON YOU IN A COUPLE HOURS STOP
GET SOME REST STOP CANNOT WAIT TO SEE YOU
STOP LOVE GUSTAVE STOP

The ticker tape was poorly glued to the marconigram paper. I flicked it with my thumb as the porter hauled my bags up to my room. The hotel was only two floors, mostly populated with oil rig and railroad workers. Many were occupying the telephone booths in the dining hall, and their eyes followed me as I made my way to the stairwell. There was no elevator. Everyone was smoking. I was the only single woman staying there, the porter exclaimed. *Except I'm not single.*

The hotel room didn't have carpeting and smelled of tobacco. As I closed the door behind me, something landed on my forearm and bit me. I slapped the skin and wiped away a splash of bug blood. The floor tiles throughout were cold. The bed had a comforter that was easily a decade old, and if you dropped a nickel into a slot, the bed would vibrate. The bathroom had black mould and the bins hadn't been emptied. But the window, albeit small, looked out over a large valley, truncated only by the railroad tracks in the distance. The power lines next to the tracks were down, stripped of their copper by thieves. Probably the reason why so many men were staying here.

With the window open, I could hear distant fox bellows. They sounded like shrieks of terror. A death knell. I closed my eyes and inhaled. Something buzzed near my ear and I swatted at it. I didn't kill it, the fast little bugger.

I showered and dozed for a couple hours, but when Gustave didn't appear, I went back downstairs. Closing myself inside one of the wooden telephone booths with a bench, I popped in a dime and called him. He answered on the thirteenth ring.

"Well, I'm here. I've come all this way," I said.

"Naseema, I'm so sorry."

"You've said that already. A million times over. What is going on? At least tell me that."

"I fucked up," he said bluntly, and I tensed up. I'd never heard him use expletives before.

"Why don't you come here and we'll talk about it," I countered softly.

"You don't understand…"

I tend to fall silent in these moments because when people don't get a reply, the awkwardness forces them to speak. You usually get the truth when you fall silent.

Gustave stayed silent for what seemed longer than

1,800 seconds, and I began to go over my precisely portioned thoughts, when he finally told me he'd gotten a nineteen-year-old girl pregnant. He didn't tell me her name or when it happened. He said she wasn't an Arab and sang at the Rusty Anchor every Thursday and Friday.

I hated myself for losing my composure, especially as the porter kept walking by the booth's glass door every five minutes or so to smile and wink at me. My nose began to sting and my chin collapsed. If I spoke, Gustave would hear my voice crack, and for the first time, I understood what Ma was trying to say that night at the dinner table. I thought about her warning, my mind screaming at me to pull myself together.

"Will you please just come here so we can talk?" I finally eked out.

"What do you think I should do?" he asked.

"What do you mean, what do I think you should do?" I barked. "I'm going to leave and you can do whatever you want."

I instantly regretted saying that. People say you should fight for what you want, so I wondered if I should be fighting to keep him. Waves of embarrassment broke like hives across my skin as I thought of having to tell my entire family that the engagement was off, after fighting so hard to get them to like a white Québécois man with a jaw that could cut glass.

"Will you come and talk to me, please?" I whispered into the black receiver.

After a long pause, he said softly, "I'm not coming."

GUSTAVE HAD PAID for the hotel room, so I stayed the full weekend. At twenty, I had been the youngest of all my cousins to get engaged. And I was engaged to someone who didn't have two hairy caterpillars for eyebrows smeared across his face. Engaged to someone who didn't have to shave his shoulders. Someone who looked...the way you're supposed to look.

But every time I almost gave in to the indulgence of crying, something would buzz in my ear. Looking up from my pillow, I saw a host of small, winged bugs on the bedpost. Fruit flies. I followed the trail: they'd mated and reproduced inside the leaky sink drain. They were everywhere. Buzzing in my face, dive-bombing into my many cups of tea, whizzing in my ear. I took the hotel slippers and whacked them with the hard bottoms, cracking them in two. Small black and red smudges stained the taupe walls.

I would think of betrayal and pain and the overwhelming loneliness of an empty and unconsecrated bed, and then I'd kill three bugs with one slipper.

I'd berate myself for being so stupid—How could I have missed the signs? How come the light bulb just never went on?—and I would clap my hands and wipe a dead fruit fly on the tabletop.

I'd wonder if, at this age, I even knew the difference between love and infatuation, and then I'd pour boiling water from the kettle down the sink, dissolving the flies and their tiny little eggs.

I stripped down naked so the dead bugs wouldn't collect in the folds of my blouse and pulled my hair back into a tight braid. The walls reverberated with every smack of the slippers. It echoed across the tiled floor and down the corridor to the other rooms. I whacked the bathroom mirror so often it cracked. Perhaps I went a little mad. Holding a slipper in each hand, I stalked the flies. As they gathered in gaggles on the ceiling, I slowly climbed atop the bed and slapped them to death.

When the walls were covered in dozens of bloody black smush marks, I screamed, "C'mon, you little sons of bitches! I fucking dare you!"

Late at night, while the foxes beyond the window shrieked under the velvet-black sky, I stood in front of the wardrobe mirror naked and really looked at myself. My body seemed suddenly to me like a very ferocious thing indeed.

Inside, something expanded and bloomed like a bell-flower, then swelled and dampened. A hip swayed, snakelike, and my belly danced, my breasts bounced.

Clapping my hands, I stomped a foot and slithered my spine in and out, overtaken by a blood fever. Ribs tightened, arms weaved, my hair flipped over my eyes, blinding me. My body seemed to sear from the lack of fingerprints marking my skin. And I wondered if, one day, I would be able to picture the face, the nose crinkles, the crooked teeth, and the soft hair of the person truly meant to love me. Will he know me the way I already know him? How long must I wait for him to capsize and drown in me?

THE FRONT DESK clerk told me as I checked out on Monday morning that Gustave had called a few times, but the porter was afraid to deliver the messages, what with all the banging and screaming. Before I could let that information go to my head, I read a marconigram Gustave had sent. It wasn't an apology, or a sad goodbye lament filled with forlorn regret. He wanted the ring back.

Halfway back to the Portage la Prairie airfield, I stopped the taxi at the main shopping strip in town and asked the driver to wait while I went to the local jeweller. He wore a small magnifying glass eyepiece attached to a headband, and his shop smelled of toast and sour milk. He told me my platinum ring with the single-carat diamond was worth quite a bit, about a month of Gustave's salary. So I exchanged it for a pearl ring cradled by two sapphires in a gold setting.

As I stepped outside, the sky sagged with rain. Some kids were doing cartwheels on the grass across the street. Their bodies twirled. Their feet reached unknown heights. Their hair bounced. Their bellies danced.

The sun peeked through the murkiness. I flicked the body of a dead bug, bloody, off my shoulder.

Back in the taxi, I asked the driver to turn up the radio. Nancy's sultry voice bellowed, as her song about the boy who shot her down, and didn't even lie when he said goodbye, came to an end.

THE LAST CIGARETTE

1978

THE DAY HE MET her started a bit hectic. He had to catch the train to Lamezia—not an all-day journey, but he knew to pack a lunch. Two cheese and pepper baguettes and a pear. There was work in Lamezia. He could hire from the trades to do the heavy labour, as he was now the general contractor, but the site needed to be inspected, work itemized, calls made, contracts signed.

He got up, ran a comb through his fading hair, and made coffee in a Bialetti, washing it while it was still hot. The pipes in his building were from the turn of the century: air was trapped in them; summer heat warmed the air, and whenever a faucet was turned, a bath was drawn, or the commode was flushed, the pipes squealed and vibrated like a howling beast. He often wondered if there truly was an ogre zigzagging though the walls of his flat. Maybe it was him.

He put on his tweed travel jacket, but he couldn't wear his favourite leather slip-on shoes anymore because of his bunions and corns, not to mention his good-for-nothing knee. So sneakers it was, per the doctor's orders. He thought he looked ridiculous. The train attendant on the platform, a young woman with painted nails, helped him up into the carriage and to his seat.

"Thank you," he said to her, sitting down. "It's my knees, you know..." He wasn't sure if she heard him because she said nothing and walked away briskly.

He had a single seat by the window, and the train hugged the Calabrian coastline the entire way. His view consisted of glimpses: A nonna hanging shorts on a clothesline. Birds circling a steeple. Aqueduct ruins. Endless stretches of beach, empty except for an unleashed dog here, a woman in a string bikini reading a book there. Then the train would hurtle through a mountainside and it all would go quiet and dark for a few moments.

At each stop, people got on and got off. Hardly anyone was alone. Two young girls with just purses came on and read magazines. A husband-and-wife duo napped, her legs slung over his. Two men in suits boarded for just one stop, talking in the vestibule about whatever it is men in suits talk about, before alighting after only ten minutes. At one station that seemed abandoned, a custodian pushed a horsehair broom across the empty platform. Occasionally, the ticket taker would come through the carriage with the hole-puncher and date-stamp. But for the most part, people seemed to take the train without ever paying for a seat.

He had bought his ticket a week in advance and kept it neatly flat and uncreased in a folder. Every morning he looked at it, so as to remember all the details. 7:00 a.m. departure. Car 6, seat 51. *Check the departures board for platform.*

He watched as everyone around him in the carriage chatted or enjoyed the scenery. Something thudded inside him. A pang that made his hands sweat. The doctor said he had a murmur, but that wasn't it. Drawing a deep breath, he picked up his duffle bag and brought out the first of his sandwiches and a mechanics' magazine. With each stop, he hoped something might save him from the quietude of his own mind. A word had to crack through the voluminous stillness.

As a boy, he always had people to talk to. Too many, in fact. He wasn't Italian back then. His mother and father had sent him down the Mediterranean to apprentice as a teenager with an electrician and drywaller. If he kept his mouth shut, no one in Sicily could tell he was Syrian. Everyone was just a different version of the same tan. He lived with five other apprentices in a two-bedroom flat. He couldn't belch without bumping into someone's elbow while another gave him hell for his manners. He was around other labourers all day, sweating and puffing in the Sicilian sun, building market arcades or townhouses for the new developments. While that kind of companionship was tiresome, he did enjoy the company of a girl now and then. One or two, he might have even loved. But he wasn't Sicilian; he had no family. Or so they kept telling him. As such, he never expected his affairs to last longer than a football season. Sometimes, only a football match. And maybe their mothers were right: maybe he was no good.

Looking at the married couple seated across the aisle, dozing as the sun peppered their faces, he wondered what might have happened had he found someone brave enough to marry him. He loved those first few months of seeing a girl, when he could tell his charms were working, that she was falling for him. All his bad habits somehow had the power to make her laugh. But it would take about three months for him to actually feel something in return. Something real, tangible, that he could pick up with his fingers. That's when he was done for. Feelings are rarely reciprocated, he realized, and so he learned to relish the three-month probationary period. That was where he found real happiness, and it was something not meant to hold in one's hands.

The train ride was long. He ate his cheese and pepper baguette. His seat reclined. The sun stayed on his shoulder.

At around the three-hour mark, she got on and sat across the aisle from him. She was humming Nancy Sinatra and her lips could break the nib off a fountain pen. She slung one leg over the other as she dropped her backpack in the aisle. The thing was bigger than her, like she was about to parachute. If his face were a flower, her eyes would have pollinated him.

She met his eyes, and he looked away quickly. There is nothing so caustic as a look that lasts longer than comfort dictates. Besides, if she took a good look at him, he suspected she'd find something repulsive. How could she not? Outside the window, antiquated ginger-coloured stucco facades lined the cobblestoned streets of whichever village this was. The village flashed only momentarily beyond the window, and then was lost behind them.

The scent of tobacco hung in the air. Men and women alike blunted their cigarettes in the aisles with their soles, but the smell lingered. Feeling the urge, he reached for his pack of smokes in his pocket and fumbled with his Zippo. Damn thing. It wasn't short on fluid; his hands just hurt sometimes. Like his knees.

Suddenly, there were two small and slender hands reaching in front of him for the lighter.

"May I get that for you?" she said. In Arabic.

In that moment, he was so tense, he could have bitten off the end of his cigarette with his asshole. He stared at her, bewildered, as she shook the lighter and flicked the flint. He leaned forward into the flame and sucked. The Zippo snapped shut with a flick of her wrist.

"How did you know I..." he asked in Arabic, pulling the cigarette from his lips.

She just smiled.

The audacity, it amused him. It also intimidated him, leaving him scrambling for a reply. Silence stings when it has been suspended. He extended his pack to her. "You want?" He was certain she didn't smoke. *You idiot.*

"But it's your last one," she said.

"It's okay. Take it."

"Some people believe you should never give away your last anything."

"Well. That's not my belief." He smiled, exhaling smoke through his nostrils.

"Funny, it's not mine either."

She put the cigarette between her lips and leaned forward. With his cigarette still in his mouth, he leaned in, sucking so the tip would turn bright orange, and brought it to her tip. Her cigarette burned.

"Now you've got me wondering," she sighed after her first puff, "how much of you I can take before there's nothing left."

He blinked. Flicked his cigarette. The invitation hung in the space between them.

"Might I ask," he began, "why would a young lady like you wish to smoke?"

Her eyes met his. "It keeps me indifferent."

~

THEY UNDRESSED AND everything happened too quickly. He could hurt someone, it had been so long, so he was very careful. He decided quickly that she was something else. Something that could send him reeling. He vowed to kiss her afterwards, and even to hold her hair back if she vomited. He was strange and sick that way.

His room in the boarding house in Lamezia was in disarray. Toaster crumbs were stuck at the bottom of the element, charcoaling; the parquet floor squeaked; the staticky radio hummed all day, flicking in and out of service. The room was cheap, but it was warm and close to the train station.

He asked her so many things that night, as she tucked her cold hands under her haunches. How could it be she was unmarried? Did she find Italy to her liking? *Why me?* She didn't answer much and kept closing her eyes as a way to end the questioning. He learned she might go to the Carnevale di Ivrea to throw oranges next. Once, she was engaged, she said, but it didn't work out. She learned to belly dance from her aunties. She kissed his snaggletooth when he smiled, then put her hand on his belly and offered him this: "My mother back home in Montreal told me that things that are unsaid should be left unsaid. It is the tension that defines us, after all."

He didn't know what that meant, but he nodded like he did. If he ruled a kingdom, he would trade it all for a modicum of her indifference. Her fingers played with the white curls around his navel. In bed, he fit effortlessly into the curves and nooks of her frame. He wrapped his arms around her torso and rested his forehead against her delicate hairline. There had been so many moments in his life, he mused, where he was a fool. He squandered his youth, he grew too old too quickly, he never let anyone get too close. His mother in Damascus would write him letters, begging for a grandchild. She taught piano and never forgave him for refusing her teachings. He swam in regrets. But for that moment, his knees didn't hurt. He wasn't embarrassed by his white hair or big belly. Something about her dark, quiet manner made him feel warm.

On the radio, a news report announced the little mill stream just north of the city had broken its banks and poured itself away over the lower vineyards into the river. The damage to the vines was substantial but salvageable, according to experts. As she dozed, he counted the beauty marks that collected between her shoulder blades: eight. He fell asleep with her warm stream of breath on his cheek. As he slept, she slipped out under the rising alabaster moon. She was morning, in a world of midnights.

∼

A YEAR LATER, a telegram addressed to him arrived at the boarding house in Lamezia. The matron forwarded it to him in Sicily.

She was getting married after a brief courtship. But it was his.

No, don't come to her, she begged. No, please don't interfere. After the life she'd had, she was repulsed by big romantic gestures. She had once flown a great distance to confront her ex-fiancé, she explained. That disaster taught her one thing: only the selfish survive, so long as they can maintain their indifference.

So every year he sent her money. It wasn't much, but it would do. The banks couldn't convert his lira to dollars in a timely fashion, so he had to convince Western Union to make the transaction, even though he didn't have the proper papers or identification. Sometimes he attached a note. *How are her grades? Does she still go to church? Please send me an updated photograph. The one I have is so old and tattered.*

She never sent a new photograph. Sometimes she would reply with a thank-you note. Most years, not. He kept her short missives in the top drawer of his dresser.

If he let himself think too much about his child, his stomach would flip, like it was slamming a door.

He continued his life in his own little world. Work was good, even at his age. It was a good grift, being a builder. Everyone from Palermo to Tropea built their single-level villas with the hope that, one day, they could add a second, so he left the rebar sticking out the tops of the columns. No one ever questioned it, *the rebar will come in handy*, they said. Rebar rusts in the rain, though. Walls with rusted rebar tend to crumble after about a decade. So he knew he'd be back, ledger in hand.

His back was strong; it was his knees that couldn't take much of a load anymore. Sometimes he looked at himself in the hall mirror after a bath, dripping, with suds still clogging his ears, and he didn't recognize his body. Where once black hair swirled atop muscles, now white drooped over a swollen belly. His toenails were the colour of tile mildew and they curled under, splitting easily. His snaggletooth ached in his jaw. Some days, he wanted to take pliers to it and crack it in half.

He now needed spectacles, and when it was too hot, as Sicily often was, beads of sweat would slide his specs down his nose. He was constantly pushing them back up. Every morning he'd wake up, set the Bialetti on the element, drink his espresso, then burn his fingers washing the thing. Every night he'd bathe and the dripping tub faucet would be the only sound. Every day, between organizing concrete trucks and yelling at lazy labourers on the telephone, he'd pause. Because he was afraid of the next day, of later, of new feelings, fresh, sharp, and hurting. They sprang up like vines in the branches of his blood.

~

ONE DAY, after one decade had turned into another, there was a longer-than-usual thank-you note. Except it wasn't from her. It was from his daughter. Of course, she wrote, she had always known. It wasn't a secret. But now that her mother was divorced, her life seemed adrift. Her message seemed less like a hello, and more like an invitation.

He folded the telegram back along its demarcated lines, slipped it into a drawer, and slowly backed away until his shoulders hit the rear wall.

He could finally see her, after all this time. The prospect of just looking into her eyes, which might be his eyes, was too much.

He could leave behind the grifting and the long days on construction sites and the muck of Sicily. Maybe he could even start again, in Montreal. He could finally tell his mother that she might find her next piano student in the family. A pang shocked his knee just then, and he fell hard like a stone. The floor tiles were cold, but his knee felt aflame, like it had been pulled from the cap, and then jammed back into place. Ligament and bone sheared against nerves, crushing everything.

As he winced and beads of sweat trickled down his temples, he turned his head and looked out the window. His flat faced the inner courtyard. Past the pulley drying lines where white linen, undershirts, sock garters, and tablecloths flapped like flags, a caterwaul pierced the air. Its echo bounced off the building walls, then was gone. The sound, for him, seemed to go on forever.

He closed his eyes. He had a terrific urge to smoke. Certain trees, like poplar and eucalyptus, still smoulder long after their fires have been extinguished. Just like the lilacs that continue to drink, even as they're dying. But he knew full well that his smoking days were over.

FAIRVIEW MALL

1995

WHEN I CAME BACK from swimming lessons Bita called to ask if I'd like to join her at the mall. It was a hot Canada Day, school was out, and her mom could drive us.

"Do you want to go see a movie at the Cineplex upstairs?" I asked. "Maybe *Pocahontas*."

"Let's just go shopping," she said.

I'd never been shopping without my mom.

I knew Fairview Mall pretty well. The rapper Snow grew up in the townhouses behind it. I spent a lot of time in the Coles and the WHSmith bookstores that sat side by side on the upper level. Saw a couple movies with my mom and sister when we first moved to Toronto from Montreal, like *Heart and Souls* starring Robert Downey Jr. and *Speed* with Keanu Reeves. My homeroom teacher was friends with Keanu; he was from Toronto, too.

My mother's husband, who was not my father, left the

year before. Since then, my sister, Arshia, had become distant. He was her father. She rolled her eyes in this fantastically cool way and spent all her time in her room doing sit-ups and not eating. That summer she worked as a salesgirl at the Limité store on the ground floor of the mall. She came home wearing the nicest skorts and one-shoulder numbers.

Bita's mom picked me up in their Ford station wagon. It smelled like wet dog; a pine air freshener from the gas station hung off the rear-view mirror. Bita was in the backseat wearing a tight tee that had 55 in fat glitter emblazoned across the chest. A metal-studded leather belt held up her men's Levi's. Liquid eyeliner gave her a cat-eye. I wore a frumpy T-shirt I had quickly pulled out of the dryer that said *Blue Jays 1993 Champions* in bright blue and bicycle shorts from Sears. I couldn't figure out why Bita had called me. She'd never really hung out with me that much at school. She knew I was being bullied. When Craig or Justin called me hairy, she smirked.

Bita's mom dropped us off in front of the food court entrance. Sitting under the skylight at the tables bolted to the linoleum floor facing the elevators to the upstairs Cineplex was a group of people Bita approached.

"Azurée," she introduced me, "this is Behzad, Charbal, Behrad, Kiana, Pooyah, and Ariel."

I'll never remember their names, I thought. I sat down

tentatively, as Bita, a shining beacon of Persian popularity, sat comfortably. I watched as she laughed and flirted with the tableful of mall rats like my sister did with the guys in her grade. Bita brought a vial of lip gloss out of her purse, dipped her pinky in, and smeared it delicately across her lips. I didn't even have a purse.

She ripped off a TTC student ticket for me—"So you can get home later"—and I stared at it like she'd just given me the key to Narnia. Bita was, like, living a whole other life. She had this hidden life of her own making, never once letting on that she had this crew outside of school. Her version of seventeen was definitely a step above mine.

The music coming from the nearby It! Store blasted Montell Jordan's "This Is How We Do It," followed by "I Wish" by Skee-Lo.

We never went shopping that day.

THE NEXT DAY after swim class, Mom noticed when Bita called again.

"We go to school together," I explained, as I pinned my bangs that I'd cut myself diagonally with a barrette and smoothed the ends behind my ear with gel. "And her mom is driving us."

Mom didn't object. I knew she wouldn't. Her divorce made her a bit meek. Sometimes I hated her for that.

"Drop in to give your sister some food at work," she said, handing me a frozen container of Sito's kousa and kibbeh.

I balked. My sister wouldn't want me to drop in. She hated being around me. I shoved the plastic bag inside my Club Monaco tote, still wet from my bathing suit and smelling of chlorine.

Before Bita's mom honked her horn out front, I snuck into the laundry room and swapped out my T-shirt for one of my sister's: a crop top from Stitches with fat horizontal green, white, and black stripes. I looked like a flag with no country.

When we got to the mall, I dumped the lunch in the bin.

THE WEATHER GREW hotter and hotter, but I wasn't riding my bike every day like last summer. I spent less and less time outdoors. Summer, but no tan. Summer, but no beach. Summer, but no rollerblading. No sitting in front of Mac's Milk and sucking on a cherry Popsicle, breaking it in two— one half for me and one for my sister. No trips to Canada's Wonderland to ride the Minebuster or Jet Scream coasters. No father figure buying funnel cakes and no Mom packing a picnic of toasted tomato sandwiches with mayonnaise and black olives.

On every street, patios were blaring Mariah Carey's "Fantasy" or the club hit "Memories" by Netzwerk. I failed my lifeguard test at the pool, so I stopped swimming.

Movies were selling out at the upstairs Cineplex, but I never saw *Braveheart* or *First Knight* or *Clueless*.

But I did hang out at the food court. Almost everyone was Persian, like Bita, and disappointed when I told them I was Lebanese. Despite hours spent in the food court, not much was eaten.

Behrad took to me to the baby changing room and tried to kiss me. I'd never kissed a boy outside of a dare back in Québec, and I think the guys sensed it. Behrad was tall, a bit pudgy in the middle, but he had a five-o'clock shadow every hour of the day and wore black turtlenecks with white jeans. He looked like a Parasuco model. All the boys I knew at school had smelly, shaggy hair and sang Adam Sandler songs from *SNL* just so they could make the fart noises in unison.

Everyone stood outside the baby changing room, listening. I wouldn't let him kiss me, but I wanted to brag to my sister. He was twenty and I was seventeen. My sister was always telling me I was a waste of skin. *But look at my crew, and the boys who like me.* He got frustrated when I kept pushing him off me with a nervous laugh, so he made silly smooching and groaning noises close to the door.

Back at the food court, Ariel, the one white girl in the group, who was chubby like me, asked me to tell her everything. She took pleasure in twenty-year-old Pooyah telling her how beautiful she was. She was sixteen.

"We didn't kiss," I said.

She laughed. "Whatever."

When Behrad's friend Sina tried to touch my leg later, I swatted at him like his hand was a hissing gnat.

"Slut," he muttered under his breath.

BITA STOPPED GOING to the mall—her mom grounded her for sneaking away at night to make out with a seventeen-year-old guy who had his own car. Bita said her brother caught her in the act in the Mac's Milk parking lot.

So Ariel started calling me. We never said anything on the phone except "See you at the mall at three?" "Okay."

Every day it was the same. She never asked me about Montreal. She didn't know about my mother's divorce. She didn't know my real dad lived overseas. And I never felt compelled to tell her.

I got black platform boots. Black jeans. Men's Levi's 501s. Tight tops from Stitches for $9.99. Dark lip liner with a nude lip colour. Sometimes I'd put glittery eyeshadow from the '70s that I found in my mom's makeup kit over the lipstick to create a matte look, and I got a lot of compliments on it. But the eyeshadow tasted like chemicals and stuck to my teeth. I stopped going to Coles or WHSmith. I never tried to retake my lifeguard test. I plucked my Arab eyebrows within an inch of their life.

One afternoon this Greek guy, George, bought a McChicken and sat with us. It was the first time anyone had ever bought food. He found a hair in it, so he complained, and when he came back with a free one, we all bought combos, then put our own hairs in them to get free seconds. Mall security kicked us out and made sure to kick us out often.

When we'd get our daily boot out of the food court, we'd go up to the Cineplex lobby to play arcade games or endless rounds at the gitoni table. The Persian guys started slicking their hair back with gel and tying it into a little tail. The girls gelled their hair until it crunched. They wore Revlon's Toast of New York on their lips and heavy CoverGirl foundation that made their faces white. The boys all wore wifebeaters; some were sheer or had fishnet patterns. Baggy jeans held up by metal-studded leather belts. One guy—Rico—claimed to be in the La Familia gang, but he wasn't Spanish. He was from Armenia.

Mom went to work, came home, and cooked. We weren't close. Arshia hated me for biting her style and embarrassing her in front of her friends. So my mall days continued into the night, sneaking into after-hours locales. I didn't know what after-hours were exactly, but they felt like a playground for boys where girls were wall decoration. One time, Ariel let Pooyah feel her up in the washroom. She gave him a hand job, and then told me later how she felt like she had no choice. I was really uncomfortable as she spoke. I was still fast-forwarding through the kissing scenes in movies we rented from Rogers Video. I didn't like people touching me. Touching seemed so one-sided. Guys liked to do it, but I didn't like how it felt. But then I would be overcome with sympathy, like I didn't want to hurt their feelings and say no. It was over quickly anyway. I kind of got where Ariel was coming from, but secretly, I started to hate her.

I started to wonder if maybe I liked Behrad. He had a blond girlfriend, so he'd never go for someone like me. But he flirted with me, and one time he grabbed my nipple through my shirt when I wasn't looking, so he must like me.

A boy from Afghanistan with green eyes named Ali Curly sat me on his lap once at the mall and stroked my hair. His name wasn't really Curly. I asked him if he'd ever had a girlfriend. He said, "Of course! That's a stupid question. Have you ever had a boyfriend?"

I was worried he would start looking at me like Craig and Justin did at school. "Yeah," I lied. "I guess it was a stupid question."

He bought me a Big Mac combo and we sat in silence, eating. I wanted to flirt with him but had no idea what to say. Sesame seeds from the bun stuck to the tiny hairs on his lip.

At the after-hours, he fingered me. He was rough and it hurt. I had fast-forwarded through too many sex scenes to know what to do, or that I was expected to like it. I froze like he was performing a root canal. Afterwards, he left and hugged all the girls goodbye except for me.

Charbal called me to talk on the phone in the evenings. He was soft-spoken and played on a soccer team. He was passionate about the sport and loved wearing his team uniform off the field. He was tall, with bleached tips and nice eyes. One time in the food court, I can't remember what I was blathering on about, but when Sina interrupted me, Charbal told Sina to wait a second so I could finish speaking. That was the first time that had ever happened to me. Then at an after-hours in Scarborough, Charbal tried to ask me out as we slow danced. I think that's what he was trying to do. I'd never been asked out before. If I assumed that's what he meant, would that make me, like, full of myself? I giggled but didn't know why. Nothing was funny. I wrote my phone number on his arm. He was Persian, but his arm hairs were blond and reflected the light.

When he called there were long silences. I couldn't think of anything to say again, and neither could he. Fingering is one thing, but awkward phone conversations are a different brand of torture.

I said, "This conversation is boring." I thought it was funny.

He never spoke to me again. Ariel told me later he'd really liked me, and I'd embarrassed him. I didn't know any of that. I didn't want any part of that. I kept stewing over that information when *Pocahontas* came out on VHS. I watched the musical number "Colors of the Wind" over and over again, rewinding specifically to the part where Captain John Smith lies down next to Pocahontas on a circle of sand and closes his eyes as he rests his temple against hers. *That's what I want*, I thought. Someone blond who thinks my darkness is captivating. Someone to rest their forehead against mine. Someone who would feel at peace by my side and close their eyes. Like my touch was the only thing holding them together. Not someone who called me on the phone to not talk. Charbal would never be like that. Behrad would never be like that. Ali Curly would never be like that.

MY TOPS HAD become crop tops, but I was embarrassed by my chubby tummy. Walking home from Fairview Mall, boys in low-riding cars would honk at me. They'd yell gross things. In a crop top I felt trapped. Ariel liked to wave at those cars. She enjoyed the attention. I thought it'd be cool if she got hit by a bus.

One time a car stopped and I thought the driver was asking for directions. He was in a white coupe, and he wore black. He looked like one of my teachers, and he smelled of Cool Water.

"I'm seventeen," I snapped when he asked for my number.

"What? You don't like meeting new people?" he mocked me. Then he called me a bitch and drove off.

One night, Ariel's dad and sister picked us up from an after-hours. Her sister stared at me disapprovingly from the front seat. She just stared, her whole body twisted around to look at me. She had sandy blond hair and freckles.

From the driver's seat, Ariel's dad interrogated her. "How much did you drink?" he bellowed. When she said nothing, he turned to me. "And how much did you drink?"

I felt my feet tingle with nerves. "Um, I'm seventeen. Nothing," I said.

He fell quiet. Sandy blond sister turned again to give me the stink eye. I still didn't understand the interaction hours later, when it was late at night and I was in bed, my books hidden under the bed frame. I had removed them from the bookshelf—that was another life. I replayed the scenario over and over in my mind. I didn't understand why they thought I would drink; they didn't understand why I wouldn't.

Because maybe my friends were something else, something other than me. Maybe there was something going on with the Fairview crew. Maybe I already knew what it was. They were ready to perform, and I was still in dress rehearsal.

In school they said a girl could do anything a boy could,

but Rico told me I needed to show him respect because he was a man. I called him a jerk, and he said nice girls don't talk to men like that. Maybe I was being rude? Maybe I actually should be nicer? If it was a choice between guys thinking I was nice and guys thinking I was chubby and hairy, then it wasn't really a choice.

But nice girls have to touch. And be touched. And say thank you.

My mom switched me out of my high school because I was being bullied. The principal apologized for not protecting me. I joined my cool younger sister at her French immersion school so I wouldn't lose my French. She rolled her eyes, but she did introduce me to her friends, who were way older than the both of us, who all drove cars and made sure no one gave me a hard time.

Within the first month, there was a short story contest run by the school board called The Writes of Spring, and I wrote a story called, "I'm Not a Real Persian, but I Play One on TV." I won first place and started writing for the school newspaper.

The days got colder and shorter. I never heard from Bita or Ariel or anyone from the Fairview crew again.

PART TWO

The sole pleasure in love
lies in the knowledge that one is doing evil.

Baudelaire

THE POWER OF THE DOG

1999

Arshia

I wake up, body splayed across the mattress in a starburst. Sunlight. Then rain. Then resurrected sunlight. The men on a neighbouring roof are hammering sadistically out of time. *Bang.* Pause. *Bang bang.* Pause. Pause. *Bang bang* pause. I can't stand my apartment walls and bound outside. Walk weightless through the heavy, congested streets.

A morning of furious feet. Victorian houses, wrought-iron balconies, stray tabbies, turquoise lawn ornaments, patio chaises. The shadows of leaves spin across the cement. Atwater Market bustles and hums with soft peaches, skinned trouts, and pink crinolines with black lace. The dogs on Saint-Urbain yip like the out-of-work actors I hang out with. I pass several European seniors out for a stroll, two blond kids playing with hula hoops on Rue Clark, ten friendly cats looking for a few good scratches.

I moved back to Montreal for university. McGill, just like my mother—except she studied the Byzantines and Philistines, while I study the city libertines. I'm so glad I came back, and not just because I got to escape my dorky older sister. There's nothing like an older sister you're incapable of looking up to. She would do well to go a little reckless—that slice of debauched cake is delicious.

The Avenue du Parc drumming circle drips a collective energy. The dreadlocked kids paint their skin with sandalwood, gold dust, and red hibiscus...then sweat out the colours into porous swirls as they dance. The park sways green blades, and the squirrels snap and squeal. Rue Rachel balconies are decayed hickory wood and twisted iron. Ambitious ivy festoons the dilapidated Victorian houses. Affluent front-porch hounds sop up the hide-and-seek sun. The Italians on Rue Berri hang wind chimes. The African craftsmen on Hochelaga sing to soundtracks. Sainte-Catherine is nothing but an outdoor mall, loved by millions, not for the architecture or the sunlight or the beauty in humans but for the opportunity to acquire things that do not change your life.

After hours of pointless promenades, I sit at a metal table in the posh downtown district and watch pigeons, paparazzi, and passersby. The sky sports a fighting rainbow, barely alive. I flip to the back of a Montreal weekly. Embedded in connections: *I-Spy.*

*new years eve. corner of the main and mont-royal. you boy. me
girl. loved each other's makeup. you went fetish. i went savage.
still wanna kiss? #574489*

*café olympico. fri 02/12. you: dark-haired beauty, over-worked
analyst? me: curly-haired, asked you to dance. our chemistry
was delicious. didn't say goodbye. can we connect? #607948*

*we met on our bikes on fairmount. where have you been? i'm
at waverly, 3rd floor. coffee? #658356*

*blonde on st-urbain bus. let you listen to my discman, chatted
w/your friends. couldn't stop smiling. let's meet. i'll let you try
my wu-tang style. #590986*

The sky has capsized and sags with rain once more.
I take mental photographs of things I never want to see
again—hungry dogs, garbage juice, screaming vermin.

Professor Bower

They are first-years with delusions. They all see themselves
as actors. The best actors to sweep through the department. Theatre Survey is a waste of their time; they want to
deconstruct a line, insert beats, pursue their super object-
ives, emotionally usurp their scene partners. They are
forced through my David French lectures, my analysis of

George F. Walker, my critique of *Les Belles-sœurs*. My job is a veiled attempt to weed out the self-absorbed brats. The ones who don't care for theatre. The ones who'll exploit it as a means to get famous. These are delusional kids. I hit them with reality.

She wears a flower in her hair to all my lectures. A passion flower. Mango-butter petals with emerald freckles. Ninety-nine-cent bobby pins puncture the stem, hold it in place. She wears it over her left ear. In Polynesian culture, wearing a flower over your right ear indicates you're married. Over your left ear indicates you're available. Or is it the other way around?

Obnoxious. Vying for attention. The low-cut tops, the hyena laugh, the inappropriate pseudo-intellectual responses. Dull essays. Poor attendance. Scamp attitude. Cavalier look. Failing grades.

Arshia

I don't know what to expect when I arrive at Professor Bower's house. He's offered essay help. Probably only for tenure brownie points.

Professor Bower is nothing if not a privileged Anglo Saxon. A severe, businesslike approach to theory. The diplomas shoved up his ass. An "academic," or a "scholar." He's known by both names. Among others.

Greetings

Christopher opens his large English oak door. His eyes go straight to her flower. It sits like a worn-out compliment in her raven hair. Her eyes are expectant, like a hanging punchline.

Arshia

He's spinning his wedding ring around his finger. You can always tell when a man is having a mid-life crisis. Professor Bower spins his wedding ring like he's trying to guess the combination.

"It's a pleasure to see you."

Yeah? Wait five minutes.

"How are you?"

I'm getting over a bladder infection and haven't been able to masturbate all week.

"Glad to hear it, have a seat."

I also wear a ring. Mom gave it to me. A pearl ring cradled by two sapphires on a gold band. She said she bought it for herself as a reminder of how close she once came to danger. Whatever that means. I'm just glad I have it and not my sister.

Beginnings

An affluent maple-lined street, with four-door Infinitis on carefully paved driveways. In the parlour of Christopher's

Victorian house, Arshia sinks into his forest-green leather chesterfield. From Pottery Barn. He calls it a "sofa."

"Jasmine tea relaxes the mind in preparation to receive new ideas. It's better for studying," he says.

Arshia hates tea, always has. Ever since someone made her Orange Pekoe after a day of figure skating in grade five. It tastes like lawn clippings in a mug.

Christopher doesn't own mugs. Only china cups.

I'm a guest at a professor's house, so I guess I've gotta suck this tea down.

She's fidgeting on my sofa.

Even if I hork on this shit, I'm gonna gulp it down for him.

She better not spill.

A few dozen sugar cubes, please. Some honey. Anything?

I prefer one good piece of furniture to a house full of Sears junk. Don't ruin this piece for me.

How long is he going to stare at me like this?

Outside, rain taps Morse code on Christopher's stained-glass windows. From their view, Arshia cannot see the homeless, Place Ville Marie, the déps, the Lachine Canal that fills the centre of the city like bone marrow.

The Power of the Dog

"The most intense scene is between Sorge and Ilona. Write this down: The destructive passion consumes him, but she is numb to any emotion. The war had deadened her sense of self. The fire in him is not reflected in her, and for expressing his desire, she makes him suffer through it. Hence the title of this scene, 'a degree of suffering is required.'"

"Professor Bower, I think the deal with 'a degree of suffering is required' is the attraction of opposites, to put it simply. The play really focuses on people bending themselves into pretzels... um, physically, psychologically, morally... you know, to survive the machinations of those in power over them."

Arshia

He looks at me like I'm a Sherwood Forest outlaw. He reflects, deliberates, ponders, contemplates. I politely sip his tea.

"Continue," he finally says.

"Uh, Sor-Sorge senses his abandonment of the party. Ilona is terribly attracted to his incredibly powerful will. Because her survival mechanism has been to accept anything and give value to nothing. S-so his committed will is very attractive, in part because it's the opposite of her own way of surviving. He has substance, and that's beautiful but dangerous."

Professor Bower repeats quietly, "He has substance, and that's beautiful but dangerous."

"She believes that 'if you have substance, you can be

broken,' right? So she just does and accepts everything in order not to be broken. She uses sex when it's necessary. She sleeps with German monsters and Russian monsters—it makes no diff ... uh, difference. As long as she can survive.

"Sorge is attracted to this emptiness. It's so perfect, 'untouched by the mud of the war,' right? But while he finds it beautiful, he can't accept it, as one who lives by will, rather than its abandonment. So he can't actually accept her substancelessness, if that's a word ... And he demands love, which is substance, and she finds it really hard to ... to ... own that, and feel love, because of the danger love causes.

"By the end of the play, though, she accepts her love for him, thereby having substance, and therefore she becomes breakable. And then, she is broken."

The gold band pulls at my skin.

Professor Bower

The flower in Arshia's hair has suddenly gotten smarter. The lady behind the meat counter at Provigo wore a flower, too, in her ponytail. I watched her slice thin strips of Black Forest ham, rump roast, hickory-smoked turkey, spicy salami, peppercorn pepperoni in flowing, stream-like movements. Her fingers—bandaged. I had purchased a bag of grapes, rotisserie chicken, and was looking for a clove of garlic. A clove? The meat lady called it "garlic slivers in skin." She had angular eyebrows and a hooknose. I asked her if she was Egyptian with my out-of-practice flirtation. She pointed me in the direction of garlic. The following week, a tall man was in her place.

She Stoops to Conquer

Once, Christopher was sitting in the tech booth, calling the lighting cues for a play, when he glanced down into the audience. In the velvet black, far from the proscenium arch, he saw Arshia on her knees, servicing a man.

Arshia

Hot liquids remind me of being a kid. Wrapping my arms and legs around Mom like a monkey when our family would go for dusk walks around the West Island. Mom wore wooden clip-clop clogs. Upon crossing our screen-door threshold, we'd feast on hummus, kibbeh, and moujadara like locusts.

Professor Bower

I-Spy, intriguing premise. I never read them, of course. Mentioned to me by a work colleague. Random strangers who've crossed paths, momentarily seek a second crossing.

piknic électronik 7/19. you: long dark curly hair, white dress over black pants. me: dark shaggy hair, glasses, sitting on bench. wish we had talked #616944

Or

you: glasgow boy with dreamy green eyes. me: redhead. march 4, met you on peel. wish i had given you my number! #625077

So I thought, why not?

provigo: mont-royal/st-urb. me: wanted to know what clove of garlic was. you: egyptian-like meat-goddess, knew garlic slivers in skin. want 2 meet 4 more talk & luv of food? #519079

A month went by with an empty inbox. And there are no Egyptians at Metro.

The Day Collapses

The flower in her hair droops again. Christopher thinks it's such a silly choice. However, it does add to her ethnic flair.

"Where are you from, Arshia?" he asks like an innocent.

"Canada, born and raised." She shifts on the forest-green leather sofa, and their knees knock: his cotton pants with her nylon-encased flesh.

"No, I mean…"

Southeast Asia? Maybe the Middle East? She has a certain otherworldliness to her face.

"I'm Lebanese and Portuguese." She meets his eye with defiance.

"Really?" His eyebrows rise. "That's interesting."

"Why is it interesting?" Her lips purse.

"No reason. I didn't know the Portuguese and the Lebanese got along."

"They don't. My parents are divorced."

He starts, "Do you identify more—"

"More with my Portuguese side or my Lebanese side?" Christopher spins his ring. I spin mine.

"People always ask me this, so I don't blame you for asking, too…"

Is this a dangerous line of questioning?

"…but I've always been Portuguese, and I've always been Lebanese."

She stirs her tea with her pinky, wipes the excess on her hip, and looks away. Out the stained-glass window come the cicada calls, police sirens, and other sounds of a burgeoning summer.

But there must be a side she identifies with more.

Her tea is getting cold. How do you say tea in Arabic?

She shifts again, and her body leaves an imprint on the sofa. She rolls her eyes around in their cavities and takes in the stacks of leather-bound books on the mahogany table.

The cat hair that dances through the air and catches on her long eyebrows. The canvases that adorn the exposed brick walls. What are they—Cézannes? Kandinskys?

He follows her glance. "That's an emerging Toronto artist. David Swartz."

She blinks.

"I like starving artists as much as the next man, Arshia."

The phone rings. Christopher jumps up and out of the room like a suicidal goldfish abandoning the glass bowl. His footprints echo through the hard-wooded house. He moves stealthily out of earshot.

Christopher climbs the steep staircase. The banister is intricate with craftsmanship and artistry. It's one of the house's features that scaled his deal with the real estate agent. He sits at the top of the stairs for a long time.

Arshia

I can hear his hushed voice but can't make out the words; they are sucked into the walls. I politely sip my cold tea, but I don't want to be at Professor Bower's house anymore. I want to skip over to Crescent Street and watch the ladies with big lips try to eat soup. When they catch their own reflections in their spoons, they always "ooh" and "ahh."

My first week back in Montreal after leaving Toronto, I bought bath mats and discount pot holders at the flea market on St-Michel and Cremazie. That giant 1950s depository of unwanted junk.

As I exited and crossed through the parking lot, a well-built man approached me, desperation in his red eyes. He looked at me like a child when playtime ends. Trustingly, I let him come close, noticing too late that he was holding a knife. Pressing the blade to my throat, he spun me round and forced me to my knees. My thoughts raced—*Is he going to cut my throat? Mutilate me?* I decided, as my knees cricked on the cement, that I would do anything he asked.

I remember a horrible choking feeling. The knife nicked near my carotid artery. I wondered if this was somehow healing him.

My bath mats and pot holders were now unusable. Tossed into dark puddles. The moon smiled like the Cheshire Cat.

Mom didn't believe me when I called and told her what happened. I was wearing her pearl ring at the time. It didn't save me from danger.

I hear Professor Bower's steps descending the staircase slowly, and then he reappears around the door frame. He looks like a sore throat, aggravated and stressed.

"Everything okay?"

"My great-aunt is dead."

He grabs a framed photograph from the mantelpiece and shows her to me. Five feet tall. Strawberry-dyed grandma curls. Floral dresses she made herself with an old Singer sewing machine she bought in the forties. Husband Joe, dead twenty years prior from lung cancer. No children. Upper and lower dentures she removed at dinner. Lived in a small two-bedroom with nephew Martin, who stole from her purse. Her purse from The Bay. Her flat shoes by Tender Tootsie. Paid for Professor Bower's undergraduate degree. He didn't invite her to convocation.

I politely gulp his tea.

He slides closer to me on the chesterfield. No, the sofa. I watch as our knees knock for a second time. My flesh aches. It seethes.

"Do you want me to leave?" I ask finally. My composure is a joke.

"You can stay for a bit more." Professor Bower does not look up from his hands. His square hands. His long fingers. He folds and unfolds them in his cotton-pants lap.

"I'll tell you about my mom's divorce, if you like," I offer naively. He does not move.

A Night Broken

A delicate bronze arm reaches for the china cup. A hairy hand attempts the same. Painted nails and white knuckles collide. Organs un-palpitate for an instant as cooled jasmine tea sloshes over the gold-rimmed side. Moistness seeps through Banana Republic cotton pants. Through Pottery Barn cushions. Kleenexes are ripped from the

box. Dabbed carefully at the forest green. Do not rub in.
Dabbed carefully at the cotton pants. Strategically. Deftly.
Apologetically. Sweetly.

Maybe rub a little.

Arshia
Professor Bower grabs hold of my wrist, holding it in place
over his lap. At first, I think he'll move my hand away.
But he brings my hand down. Contact. He removes the
saturated Kleenex from my fingers, tosses it somewhere
out of range.

He makes a mess and I refuse to get another Kleenex.

Professor Bower
So she does, indeed, stoop to conquer.

Arshia
I cut through Chinatown, after picking up a university-
stamped envelope from the post office. An assembly line
of golden Buddhas, Ming vases, and brass gongs stretches
up Clark. Baskets of loose grains, slices of dried ginger,
flattened pigs' feet, husks of bok choy, jars of marigold
tamarind sauce, tubs of bamboo shoots, shimmering
sprouts. And let's not forget the fish markets. Cod, eel, trout,
oysters, salmon, sturgeon, catfish, bass, and, my favourite,
suckers—all dead and rotting slowly in the summer heat.

I walk by the suckers, their high fins fluttering in the wind, their golden quillbacks shining. Splayed open on a table, their pink insides expose an overabundance of bones and arteries, not meat. The last fish on the table catches my attention.

I stop and lean in closer. At the centre of the splayed fish is its tiny fingernail heart. Still beating.

I hold the envelope up to the light, unable to make out the laser-printed message. I rip it from the paper shell as shop owners and mothers bicker over prices all around me.

A two-thousand-dollar academic scholarship.

I shield my eyes from the sun. The sky is blue. The kind of robin's egg blue that worries you because you know it'll never hatch. It's dead inside.

But then it does hatch, and you wonder what to do next.

A DEGREE OF SUFFERING
IS REQUIRED

2003

ONE OF MY university professors told me that Yoko Ono masturbated while recording one of her albums. Apparently, at first all you hear is the displacement of air, but as the needle scratches the vinyl, Yoko's orgasm grows in intensity, becoming a stentorian roar. Then, after the climax, a deep silence. My prof went on and on about how Yoko was expressing her sexuality as a woman, as a human being. Exposing her private vulnerabilities to an unforgiving culture. All I wanted was the CD.

HMV doesn't carry it, but I did borrow Yoko Ono's book *Grapefruit* from the library. Flipping through it, I found myself staring at a black and white photo of Yoko sitting dishevelled on a wooden floor at Carnegie Hall in New York, 1965. (I wonder if that same floor is still there now.) Her clothes were torn—no, cut. She held musmahtahs precariously over her breasts. The caption explained that after she first performed *Cut Piece* in Kyoto in 1964, she sat on the Carnegie stage with a pair of scissors. She invited the audience to take the scissors and cut away her clothes at any point, taking the sliced cloth with them.

I tried looking into Yoko's reprinted photocopy eyes, her expression frozen forty years ago. But she wasn't facing the camera, and it was snapped at such a distance, I couldn't read her at all.

A few lines down, Yoko said something like she felt the audience wasn't merely cutting her clothes; they were cutting away parts of her they hated, until only the stone of her being was left, whatever that means.

I put the book down and watched a Japanese woman flipping through a travel book a few stacks down pretend she didn't see me staring. If I had been in the Carnegie audience that night, I would have scraped the tip of the scissors blade against Yoko's skin. I would have made her bleed.

ONCE, WHEN I was about fourteen or fifteen, I didn't know I was bleeding, though twenty-eight days had passed. Forgot to check my calendar. Kensington Avenue, a crowded Saturday, a short skirt. Blood was drooling down my legs, staining my socks, leaving a menstrual river on the cement; I felt like a child in a twisted version of "Hansel and Gretel." When a stranger finally pulled me aside and clued me in, I found I had doused half the market in my DNA. My genealogy. I wasn't embarrassed. More like flushed, dizzy with elation. My ethnicity was bleeding out.

Kensington Market, where the wind stinks of dried pig's feet and cantaloupe incense, transformed from an urban punk neo-hippie district to my blood supplier. Blood on the avenues of Baldwin, Augusta, and Kensington, where the tunes of Radiohead, Peaches, Aphex Twin, and Hawksley Workman envelop the alleys. The century-old picket fences around Victorian front lawns are redecorated yellow and turquoise, the crinolines are worn as skirts, and nylons are worn as hats. The trees twine around the lampposts, the stray tabbies sleep in discarded mufflers, and Che Guevara fights a revolution from his one-hundred-percent-cotton eyes. In toy soldier–lined shops, a plethora of fruits, pickled goods, sauces, and chewy candies trick my bloodthirsty senses. Pickled beets, guava halves, peeled Roma tomatoes, spiced and curried honeys, over-ripened lychees, plum tapioca, pomegranate seeds, raspberry balsamic vinaigrettes, Québec maple syrup, skinned kiwis, corn syrup, roasted pears, black-currant jam, A1 Steak Sauce, pumpkin seed toffee squares, sweet teriyaki sauce, red pepper juices, Sola Nero wines… each of these are five-sense tricksters. If I eat them, it's like I'm ingesting blood. My favourite activity is squishing the peeled Roma tomatoes in my fist, letting the juice weep down my arms, dripping off my elbows. The smooth red membranes disassemble and web themselves between my fingers. An orgasm, small but significant, follows.

I lifted my skirt and hooked my thumb around my undies. The thick viscosity of my menstrual blood felt like squeezing a jelly candy between my fingers. Squishy. Its bubbles popped and spurted as I lifted globs of it up to the light. The intensity of my ancestors was all at once illuminated: the ones who left Lebanese sweat on the stone steps of the church in Montreal while washing them; the ones who never left Damascus—their muscle pain from carrying grain sacks from the market, their wrinkles from watching the village swell with age, their blindness from staring into the midday desert sun, their hoarseness from singing a traditional chant.

The red staining my fingers looked better than a jelly candy, I decided. I opened my mouth and sucked it down. Bitter. Like a salty tea bag soiling my palate. I licked my fingers clean. I felt closer to Jido. I could taste him.

I never knew Jido. Ya haram. He died when I was a baby. Sito came to live with us in Toronto years after we left Montreal, and suddenly Mom remembered all her Arabic. They almost never spoke it around me. Said they didn't want me to know what they were talking about. Ma behkiin arabiin.

I didn't speak Arabic as a child. I would hear Mom and Sito yakking back and forth in it, their spittle shooting across the kitchen, as they made yakhnet batata imfariki and moujadara and fattoush. The nuances of this gastro-intestinal language were lost on me, how their guttural expectorations were considered sentences. Of course, like any language, you learn the swear words first. Elhassi tizi (they still won't tell me what that means) and q'iss imik (I think that has something to do with female genitalia) and ouij'ic mittl uhti (again, female genitalia) and dami fowr'ik (that means "May your blood boil over," but it really loses potency in translation).

Sito is crazy, and I'm in love with her craziness. She's the only person I've ever met over eighty who likes the profanity of "motherfucker," who sits cross-legged on the floor in front of the TV, who reads *Cosmo* but who, oddly, refuses to talk to me about sex.

"That's for low-class people," she says. I guess she learned "motherfucker" from Father Shaheen at Saint Nick's.

Now, Sito is twisting her thin arm behind her back, reaching for her zipper, her sandpaper skin stretching flat across bone. It's anyone's guess why she never sews zippers in to the side, or lower down her back, instead of wedged behind her neck. Sito was a seamstress in the 1940s, and now she makes her own dresses. She said she loved the boutiques near Jean Talon when she was a little girl and apprenticed with her favourite dressmaker after she married Jido. She never did open her own boutique. Having my mother being the main reason.

Red polka dots with a black background, blue polka dots with a white background. When Sito and Jido lived in Montreal, she always bought striking patterns from Fabricville in Dollard-des-Ormeaux. And in their basement sat her ancient Singer sewing machine, fitted inside a table with a huge foot pedal. She got it at a discount after years of making dresses for rich people at Madame Dineen's.

Sito likes to tell the story of her first day working for Madame Dineen. It was 1949, and Jido was still unable to work after the trauma from the war. Nervous with the pressure to support her family, a young Salma ran the sewing machine needle right through her nail. A part of it is still lodged in her finger to this day.

"Be grateful for your education," she likes to say, "because I never got one. I had to work."

Sito doesn't ask me to unzip her. She insists on doing it herself. So stubborn. She gets it eventually and slips off her V-neck dress. Picking up her green towel and her sensitive-skin soap, she declares, as she does every night, "Okay, I'm gonna take my bath, so don't use the water." Ya'lena. Night after night, year after year of hearing this announcement, I know well enough not to use the fricking water.

In a few minutes, when I hear the tub filling, I think I'll flush the toilet.

We turned our computer room into a bedroom for Sito when she moved in. I sit on her bed, where a stack of floppy disks and a hard drive once sat, and peer around her small space. Pictures of me as an eighties baby. Photos of mom in the seventies. Pictures of Jido in his forties uniform.

Sito likes to boast about how her husband was the only Lebanese infantryman in the Royal Montreal Regiment. I move closer to the gilt-framed photo of him. Smoky hair swept into a pompadour. That thin, frowning moustache, those eyes shaped like stretched almonds. A square jaw, strong neck. When I stare long enough, I get an idea of what Sito has been talking about all these years. Goddamn. Mom says I have his eyes. She says he used to love playing with me. He'd lie me flat, spread my fat baby arms apart, and tickle me senseless. Mom says the greatest tragedy is that he didn't see me grow into a woman. A fine, young Lebanese woman.

Sito's water stops running—a long, hot bath. I open her mahogany dresser drawers, rummaging through sweaters, silk scarves, nylon sockettes, gloves. I find more photos of me—in Strawberry Shortcake diapers, at my baptism, lots of boring baby crap. Then, inside an old sardine tin, I find three cubic containers. I flip them open. Slides. About twenty-five slides per container. They look ancient. Using my fudge-painted fingernails, I delicately ease one out and hold it up to the light, cover one eye. Sito is fifty-five years younger. Black hair, stained lips, smooth skin. She's standing on a Victorian front porch next to a winding metal staircase, indicating the distinctive architecture of the Saint-Denis and Jean Talon area. Next to her on the porch is a young, dark Jido: high-waisted zoot-suit pants, short-sleeved shirt, suspenders with shiny clips, smiling carbon colours.

My fudge nails trace Jido's lines and all his angles. His soft gaze. My hands are stained with his face.

THE GUY AT the photo lab with an engraved TYLER☺ name tag raises his eyebrows at my request. He's got two silver hoops in his left ear and twenty studs crawling up his right ear. I continue counting piercings—a tongue stud, a nose stud, two eyebrow rings in his right brow, a labret spike, and only he knows what else is under his over-starched shirt. With his faux-hawk, metallic painted nails, and black eyeliner, TYLER☺ looks like the type of fucker who'd do all the piercings himself, with a musmahtah full of ice and a hole-puncher. He's my kind of fucker. Imagine the blood.

My Applied Theory and Crit professor recited an Edwin Shneidman quote that resonated with me: "No one commits suicide out of joy."

What about gashing myself? I come when I click open a Swiss Army knife. The cuts habitually result in a massive release of natural endorphins. A pleasure rush of blood.

When I was seven, I took a flying leap off my backyard

swing as it soared mid-air and smashed my forehead on a tree root. Before the pain, before I passed out, before Mom screamed to the neighbours over the fence for help, I experienced what I can only describe as Never Never Land. It felt like anything and everything but what it was.

But I'm particular. Regular intervals. No razor blades or shaving instruments—too cliché. Wiltshire knives are my weapon of choice because they sharpen every time you pull them out of the holder. If I happen to be in public, where knife-wielders are usually tackled by SWAT teams, then my instrument becomes whatever's at my disposal. The blades of grass in the park, discarded bricks at construction sites, table edges or plastic fork tines at the mall food court (but never the knives; they couldn't cut through hot hummus), paperclips, fountain pen nibs, sewing needles, my jeans' zipper, sharply angled statues, portable-fan blades, those plastic clips for bread bags . . . One time, I even used the delicate pages from the Book of John. Divine.

I never cut the same spot in one week. I like a sense of symmetry with my scars. If there are two on my right upper thigh, then there must be two on my left lower calf. One on my left nipple, then one on my right shoulder blade. Fresh wounds don't bleed as much as fresh scabs. Ripping scabs is like popping pimples or plucking stray hairs. They beckon.

"These slides are over half a century old," TYLER☺ rudely breaks into my inner monologue, shuffling through the cases. "Transferring them onto photographic paper is—"

"Can you do it?" I ask, noticing how he's freely staring at my breasts. My inner knife blades open.

He straightens his back. "Yeah, I can do it, but . . ."

"Great. Call me when it's done." I stampede to the exit.

"It won't be cheap!" he yells after me.

I slam the door chime as my response. I imagine the Wiltshire knife in my rib cage scraping away at the inside of my heart until it's red and seething, rigid and raw to the touch.

SITO'S AT THE STOVE making laban and loubyeh imfariki with her back to me, so I slowly open my purse. The photographs came back, and aside from the fact that they're in black and white, there's nothing antiquated about them. They look like they could've been taken yesterday. There's one of Sito and Jido when they were newlyweds. Sito standing on the wooden porch of their first home on Rue Berri in Montreal. Jido leaning off the black, winding metal staircase. In a white short-sleeved shirt, black suspenders, and black pinstriped pants that reach above his navel, my twenty-six-year-old jido has his arm around my twenty-two-year-old sito in a polka-dot dress that ties around her narrow waist, and he's planting a sloppy kiss on her cheek. She has a hand on his enveloping arm and is smiling through a laugh, a bit of her dark lipstick on her teeth. Another exposure on the porch shows Jido holding Sito precariously in his arms, her legs frozen in a swing, her face buried in his as he plants another sloppy one on her. I know Sito by the shape of her hips and the profile of her long nose.

I never knew Jido was such a lovertine. Mom used to tell me how strict he was, how she wasn't allowed to go to a Beatles concert, to sing in a rock band, to live downtown. Her parents always reminded her how close she came to marrying a disrespectful white man. Sito always describes Jido as "such a good, classy man." I never heard "raging pheromones," or "dirty jokes," or "free spirit." I just assumed that the 1930s was a time of severe, businesslike approaches to life.

There are a few more photos. Of Jido and Sito lying in a leaf mound on Mont-Royal in trench coats, and Sito posing on a balcony with pathetically primeval power lines stretching in the background. Then there's Jido's army photo again, but it's slightly different from the gilt-framed one. He's smiling.

The smell of dried yogourt, fried green beans, tahini, scrambled brown eggs, spicy onions, and coriander saunters throughout the kitchen. Sito always said Jido was the chef of the family. She knew how to prepare certain foods, like kibbeh, but "any Johnny could make that," as she would say.

"Sito, you miss Jido, right?" I say, childlike.

"Azurée, there isn't a day that I don't think of him. He was such a good, classy man." A rogue green bean rolls off the cutting board; she quickly spears it with her knife.

"Right." I gather my thoughts, inhale, and say, "Do you feel like you're forgetting some of him?"

She moves the metal spatula around the pan and spicy steam sizzles up to the range hood. "I'll never forget him."

"No, what I mean is—do you feel like you've forgotten the sound of his voice? Or his aftershave scent, or the way his eyebrows would rise, or his chewing noises? Stuff like that."

"He was the love of my life. I remember everything about him."

I feel the knife blades open within me.

"What was he like in bed?"

Sito drops the spatula.

I quickly say, "I didn't mean it that way."

She bends over slowly, her vintage muscles straining for a little flexibility, picks up the spatula, and wipes some of the spattered sauce off Mom's porcelain seafoam tiles. She goes back to her frying pan, absolutely silent.

"What I meant to ask was, did he have a big cock?"

Sito whips around. "Azurée! That's low-class talk. It's a

good thing he's not here, 'cause he'd give you a good smack in the nose," she blusters.

Then after a pregnant pause, she curses, "Q'iss imick!" Snapping off the element, she covers the pan and storms out of the kitchen, wiping her hands on her blue polka-dot dress.

I look down at the army photo of Jido. I walk slowly to the small TV next to the sink that hangs underneath the cabinets and switch it on. It's an Always commercial. I stopped wearing pads quite some time ago. Got booted out of Le Château on more than one occasion for leaking on their fall fashions. Dribbled once over a girlfriend's white bedroom carpet, was never invited back.

"Avoid messy spills and unwanted odours," says the chipper narrator. She goes on to describe the pad's features—it's a huge insole-sized pad.

With dry weave.

And wings.

And an optional sunroof.

Ya'lena. I grab a Wiltshire knife from the drawer.

TYLER☺ SITS DOWN on the oak park bench and unzips his navy Adidas jacket. He's wearing one of those novelty T-shirts that reads, *I'm just a pirate sailing the seas in search of booty!* I fold and unfold my hands in my secondhand-skirted lap. His smile is ripe as he pulls out a linen musmahtah, a bottle of rubbing alcohol, and a long industrial sterling silver needle. He looks around for a second—no one is watching. An older woman in a similar Adidas track suit is walking her muzzled pit bull, and in the dip of the park's hill is a small group of Tai-Chi-ers. The needle goes unnoticed as it moves from his hand to mine. I douse the musmahtah in alcohol, swipe it across my earlobes a couple times, and then once across the needle. TYLER☺ smells of sour mango candies.

"You do it." I put the needle back in his hand.

His eyes brighter than a cellphone display, he bums closer to me, moves his nose inches from my carotid artery. His breath inflates my shirt. His clammy left hand tilts my head up and holds it steady, while his warm right hand positions the needle lobe-centred.

"Breathe," he instructs.

A short-haired woman passes close to us, and I'm at certain it's Yoko. She looks up and darts her eyes around the scene. It's the Japanese lady from the library. She's wearing a chiffon scarf around her neck and a Burberry jacket. She moves on and away.

I finally exhale as TYLER☺ tears the needle delicately through my flesh, a thin stream of warmness running like syrup down my jaw. He slides the needle up and out and presses the musmahtah to my fresh wound. I squeeze my eyes shut as Never Never Land zips through my organs. TYLER☺ knocks his forehead against mine and shifts the saturated musmahtah to lick my piercing.

I open my eyes momentarily to hear him say, "We'll do the other ear another day," and then I drift off again.

I DOWNLOAD "(JUST LIKE) STARTING OVER" by John Lennon and Yoko Ono off the internet and turn off all the lights. Light cheap candles on the windowsill and headboard.

They're scented like raspberries and green apples and patchouli. The cylindrical shapes invert and cave in. They collapse in on themselves too quickly, within the hour. The wicks fluctuate with the mass of liquid flowing over them. The wax drools like melting icicles down my plaster walls. Their artificial scents don't mix, and the air around me smells like vodka.

I pick up one warped candle and blindly pour wax slowly over my arm. It scars my skin for seconds only, then peels off my elbow, my wrist, my shoulder like a bandage. The pain is orgasmic, and I remove my jeans and tank top. I pour green apple wax on my thighs and over my bony, hairless knees. The patchouli wax peppers my peach-fuzz belly, shifting with the rise and fall of my diaphragm. The raspberry wax covers my forehead like chocolate ganache. It blisters my blackheads and burns some hair to the follicles. It really hurts, and I giggle.

Yoko begins to masturbate. The knife blades open within me. I slip off my bra and undies and pick up the Wiltshire knife from beside my bed. Yoko moans, and I cut my breast. The blood mingles with the patchouli wax, hardening into solid shapes over my peach fuzz. Yoko moans deeper, and I join in as her Lebanese chorus. Yoko inhales sharply and exhales an "ahh."

I bring one bloody finger up to my lips as I bring an opposite waxed finger down between my thighs. Yoko and I growl through clenched teeth. She's teasing me with the idea of cutting her. Of running the scissors' blade across her breast. Of pushing our two bleeding nipples together like one collapsing raspberry candle losing its flame. My two hands encounter moist heat, and I don't know whether to cry or go blind. I look down at my wounded breast. The wax has coerced the blood to paint my body in a starburst. It feels like Jido is wrapping me in a warm scarlet blanket. I bring the Wiltshire knife between my legs.

My photos of Jido litter my room. Yoko and I begin our tearful release. Jido is holding Sito precariously in the air, her legs mid-swing, and he's planting a sloppy kiss on her face. Yoko and I yelp. Visions throb through my agonizing mind.

Of Jido's penis breaking Sito's maidenhead.

Yoko and I call out.

Of Sito's vaginal blood staining their fine linen.

Yoko and I groan in spurts.

Of Jido bending down and tasting Sito's blood.

Of the blood rushing out of my breast and body.

Of the blood rushing to my clitoris.

Of the blood rushing to my brain.

Yoko and I climax together in a long, slow exclamation. The wax on my body has cracked from my movements and crumbles like a temple onto my sheets. My body, stiff and fluid at once, capsizes and I drift between worlds. My speakers fluctuate as another song starts up.

With china-doll delicacy, I bring my hands up to my face. They are wet with blood.

My hands are stained with his face.

My lips envelop my fingertips, and the familiar taste of my lineage, for the first time, fills me like baklava. Sweet and sinful. I lick my lips.

Sito is banging on my door, and I wonder if she knows how much I love her. If Jido will forgive me for the suffering it took to get here. Azurée inti helwi. The scattered flames turn red as I close my knife blades.

BLINK

2006

I

ZAEV POURS ALMOND milk into the dip of my belly. It spatters like a starburst, but his tongue captures the overflow. I twirl my split ends around my fingertips as he orbits my pelvis, teeth scraping lightly over my flesh.

As he hooks his thumb around my panties, he murmurs into my ear, "For centuries, our women were beckoned onto the Rock of Raoushé slopes adorning the shores of the Mediterranean. They would lift up their dresses and straddle their legs over the sea. The presence of their wombs would calm the currents before the fishing boats set out for the day."

"Is that what you believe?" I look down at my fingers, which are lightly stroking their way down the tortoiseshell of his belly.

Zaev doesn't answer. Did he see me roll my eyes?

Instead, he smears my lipstick across my face. His thumb curved like a lunar crescent.

DAWN IN BEIRUT. I dress as Zaev sleeps. A white spandex halter top that cups my breasts. A maroon wrap skirt with gilt embroidery. I found them buried in the racks at Courage My Love in Kensington Market, which is thousands of kilometres away, but I can still see those silver racks. I can pick up the scent of the African incense that burns near the cash register. The owner's long-haired cat always roams quietly about my feet as I wrench open drawers of detailed stockings, bedazzled suspenders, and plastic-beaded crocodile hair clips.

Snap back to the present. Circling the room service tray, I shove three fingers of garlic hummus and tabbouleh into my mouth, suck down on my tips. Nibble on a handful of chewy black olives. Finish off the fried tomatoes. Teardrop-shaped kibbeh. Crispy simmered eggplants trickling oil. Hollowed zucchinis pregnant with rice and minced meat in stewed tomatoes. Pita triangles remain untouched.

I drop to my knees and search for my underwear. Pink with red stripes. The elastic band falls below my hip bones. They're my favourite. I wonder if Zaev is dreaming on top of them. Like the curious Kensington cat, I meander across the carpet, which scrapes my knees, to his side of the bed.

White sheets in a dead-body heap. Warm air looms in his corner, like his mouth has been open all night. His midnight body hair collects in the usual places. Around the eye of his belly button. In swirls across his thighs. Peppered at the small of his arched back. Leading down to the mouth of his spine. Zaev has gone under the pillow, his breathing thick.

Last night we fucked without closing the blinds. I imagine the people in the apartments across the decomposed street enjoyed our performance.

I woke up this morning wanting to run my fingers over Zaev's collarbone.

And then break it.

I abandon hope for my undies and slink over to the window, pull the armchair up to the pane. The day is ultrablue. The yellow-brown city swelters. The heat is flustering, even when we are asleep. Arabic prayer chants, like wailing jeremiads, echo through the narrow streets of distorted cobblestones and crumbling asphalt in the Hamra district, calling the faithful to face east. Neighbouring gelato cafés amplify the American Top 40 radio station. Palm trees necklace the curves of La Corniche, and streets the colour of gold tentacle from Place de l'Étoile, sporting haute couture for the nouveau riche in their display windows. Family-owned fruit markets sell football-sized pomegranates for only one thousand Lebanese lira each

(How many seeds did you eat, Proserpine?). Old men wearing argyle caps carry baskets of loose grain and husks on their backs. They pause to rest in front of melon vendors, paying no heed to the crumble of Roman columns the tourists are camcording all over. Large terracotta jars brandish freshly sprouting herbs.

Outside, the shadows on Mount Lebanon keep time better than a clock, a holy place to which the devout make pilgrimages. I recall the stories of Tammuz and Astarte my great-grandmother Alzira told. It was morning on the mount when Astarte first caught sight of Tammuz, unveiled herself before him, and buried his mutilated body when he was killed by a wild boar. The legend evokes the image of the earth being fructified by their passion and pouring forth an abundance of flowers and fruits, heralding the equinox.

I lean back in the chair, raise my feet, and press them against the glass. I slip my skirt up and position my womb toward the chaotic city.

II

THE MUSIC OF THE flat-tuned oud rockets through the narrow passages between the dilapidated apartment buildings. Prayers echo. Allahu akbar. La ilaha illa'allah. The reflecting rays of forty-degree sunlight throw shapely shadows around my feet. Women wear tank tops with spaghetti straps and tight-fitting clothing, but I've yet to see an exposed calf or thigh. In the ferocity of the Middle Eastern climate, all around me are jeans and slacks. Leering men, cigarette smoke, magazine vendors, dancing pigeons, cut melons, Western Bank office towers. Maronites. Druze. Orthodox. Sunni. Shoe shiners on their knees, stray cats pawing Styrofoam containers, jewelled narghiles sitting in shop windows. Saudi cloaks sold next to Armani suits. Dark hair laces around little girls' faces. Majestic postcards: Byblos, Rashaya, Tyre, Baalbek, Jounieh, Chekka.

The waiters here at the Al-Sa'a café stare at my bare legs as they adjust the seating arrangements on the patio. They don't have pistachio-almond ice cream, so I order jasmine tea instead. Back in Toronto, as we sat in a Baskin-Robbins, my friend Neve said, "I'm not surprised pistachio-almond is your favourite flavour. It's culturally appropriate. The pistachio is a Middle Eastern nut."

That particular night, as we jumped and gyrated ferociously to the arias of Metric and Bedouin Soundclash at the Dance Cave, I pumped my arms in such a swirl that I slugged Neve across the face. Really good. Instantly, I felt a current of pleasure, new and strange. Neve disappeared to put cold water on her cheek and stare at her reflection in the washroom mirror. Revellers orbited the dance floor in a nebula, disco balls and laser beams firing like comets. She returned, and over the pulsating bass, I do remember her sheepishly saying I had punched her, but I don't remember being awfully apologetic about it.

I guess I am a Middle Eastern nut.

My tea finished, the saturated green mulch at the bottom of my porcelain cup reads me a future. The leaves lace in and out, glossy with predictions.

The traffic zooms in disorientation and complete chaos. The traffic lights don't work and are hardly obeyed when they do. Vespas speed into oncoming traffic. No lane demarcations. Horns blazing like brimstone.

Downtown Beirut has returned to its glorious status as the Paris of the East. I stroll by Ottoman facades. The arrangement of the smooth sandstone structures forms an eye that stares up to Paradise. Soldiers stand in camouflage in front of gilded palaces and twelfth-century mosques. People throw their empties at ancient Gallo-Roman columns that are barely standing. Photos and banners of the assassinated Prime Minister Rafic Hariri adorn every window, his visage fading into light-damaged blues. The soaring iron monument erected in Martyrs' Square in tribute to civil war heroes is, ironically, bullet ridden. The Holiday Inn, which was erected before the civil war, still stands, but with so many ammunition rounds speckling its surface, I wonder if it's structurally sound. Penetrated. Punctured. Wounded. Disaster upon disaster. Wreckage upon wreckage.

But the Mediterranean water is so enviably blue. I amble along La Corniche in the scorch of the day and pause in front of the Pigeons' Rock, Zaev's words like a shroud over my flesh.

Over 140 years ago, my ancestors sailed away from these shores. Over 140 years later, I've returned to these shores to figure out why.

I find an internet café in the basement of a pool hall. Windows 98. The M, Q, Z, W, T, and U are misplaced across the keyboard. Trouble logging on to MSN Messenger.

You have 1 new message in your email inbox.

Kids clutch joysticks and combat digital terrorists. European journalists type Morse code into their keyboards, editorializing about Syrian troops they've never met, elections they've never witnessed. The Australian backpacker at the next terminal covertly eyes forbidden Danish cartoons. I click the light blue pop-up box that takes me into my overburdened Hotmail account.

Sent: March 1, 2006, 3:16 AM
Subject: Bénédictions
My Azurée,
When you come back, when Beirut leaves your bones cold and crunchy, I want you to disregard our age difference

145

and marry me. You don't have to love me. No sex if that prickles your spine. We don't even have to live under the same roof. I just want a guarantee that when my daughter puts me in a retirement home, which may be very soon, you'll come and visit me.

With love,

Matt

I pause for a long time amid the hum of the modem. The Australian backpacker vacates, leaving brown paper cups on the table. Cold traces of peppermint coffee stick to the insides.

Sent: March 1, 2006, 1:57 PM
Subject: RE: Bénédictions
dear matt,

that's something to think about. forgive me if i take some time to give you an answer. i feel like there are things i need to figure out here. like i'm testing myself to see what i'm made of. or am i testing others?

today, i walked in destroyed areas and tried to ignore the looks of the lazy soldiers lounging on every street corner, around every bend, and in every nook. i sauntered by the heartbroken holiday inn. the snipers really did sabotage it. no windows, no paint, only concrete, rubble, and millions of tiny entry wounds no surgeon could suture. it towers over the intercontinental phoenicia,

but it's completely hollowed. i stared at it long enough
to begin to feel the war zone effect.

i miss you tons.

azurée

Certain things in Toronto weave a delicate tapestry:
the cornucopia of yellow dresses sported on Queen Street
West, the booksellers with jangling door chimes on Bloor
Street, the spicy pasta aromas wafting from patios in
Little Italy, the streetcars that rattle down the centre of all
the avenues, and the drumming circles that whip bodies
around in Trinity Bellwoods Park. It is where Matt, my
wounded widower, buys me almond tea from the Tequila
Bookworm café and stares at me with eyes of wonderment.
Everything there is oh so pretty.

In Beirut, however, visions of lust linger inside me until
it's all I see. Want to growl on Mount Lebanon, hitting
Zaev across his gut with my fisted knuckles. Want nothing
civil about our war. Want him to endanger me with the
violence of his appetite. Want to reach inside him until
it stings us both. Until we are anointing our bodies with
sweet-smelling unguents.

III

ZAEV SHAKES HIS fist at me. I shake mine back.

One.

Two.

Three.

He has paper. I have rock. With such pride, his paper fans out into cupping fingers. We look down to our bent knees and flat thighs folding into each other. He has reached down below my pink underwear with the red stripes. His knuckles brush through my pubic hair and rest there.

"Best two out of three?"

One.

Two.

Three.

I have scissors. He has rock. He says nothing, yet I know he is smug as he allows himself to rub my Zen, like he's freeing me from desire.

"Best three out of five?" I cock my head.

"I want to ask you a question." He leans into me. I lean out.

"Don't talk," I mouth. My breathing burrows inside the stone of me, surging down to where I meet his fingers.

"I want you to tell me a secret." His eyebrows meet in the centre. So unkempt and bushy. I rearrange them with my stare.

"Are you asking me?"

"Tell me what burns a hole in there." His other hand moves to point to my chest, and it grazes over my brown nipple. My red heart.

My shoulder blades edge off the side of the bed. He comes sliding up beside me. We hang precariously on the edge. The cotton sheets make stretching noises as they hold our weight.

Last night, I dreamt that the water I swam through, crystal cyan water surrounded by light coves, was toxic to goldfish. As they dropped into the blue, they turned a violent violet and died. But they didn't float to the surface upon their demise. They sank to the bottom and disappeared into a blur of swaying weeds and sand.

Zaev's aqueous eyes are the colour of burnt copper. He has two pimples at the tip of his lip. Small and red, with dried skin crusting around them. I focus on their little eyes.

"In therapy," I staccato, "I was instructed to write a painful memory on a slip of paper, and then burn it. I never wrote mine down."

"What was your memory?" His skin is sun-roasted.

Long pause. Zaev glissandos and pizzicatos on my astral body with a familiar crescendo.

I pull my lips apart. "I've broken many bones, but none of them have ever been my own."

He then says, "You seem like you'll never want love. Only excitement, yes?"

"Love bores me," I say, but really, it just disappoints me.

Like a cat licking cream, he asks, "How do you manage this?"

"The secret is not looking back," I reply.

Zaev lifts his hands from me like they've been burnt. I am fructified, and I spill forward my flowers and fruits.

~

Sent: March 2, 2006, 8:09 AM
Subject: RE: RE: Bénédictions
My Azurée,

Thanks for writing. You give me new eyes and ears.

I know what I feel. And I'm feeling a woman with a mind and a spiritual aura and a body that has some mystery to it. I'm feeling ten thousand years of biological imperative.

I bet you're the centre of attention there. You are alive in wonderful ways. And you're fucking smart. There's no substitute for that. But please, no walking around Beirut in a halter top. Refrain from rebellious acts. My daughter, Fran, kissed her boyfriend too close to a mosque in Tunis and took a whack to the face by some mad religionist. I implore you to cover up and learn what you can about women living with the veil.

This reminds me of the day we met. You walked into my office for a job interview. I felt like I'd been hit with a bat (do they play baseball in Beirut?). I felt like everything I said to you sounded so stupid. Here's this young,

creative fireball with a riot in her heart, and I'm this old
fart, stuck behind memories and a four-foot-long desk.
Remind me why you chose me as a friend again!

    With love,

    Matt

I almost delete his email. I have spent my entire adult life
running away from men who wanted more from me, when
all I wanted was a good pair of runners to carry me along.

Sent: March 2, 2006, 9:24 PM
Subject: RE: RE: RE: Bénédictions
dear matt,
i once read that ancient egyptians wrote letters to the
dead when they couldn't find any exhilaration among
the living. does that explain us?

    i've made a friend here. the taxi driver who zoomed
me from the airport to my hotel weeks ago. his name is
zaev and he's a lebanese jew. exceptions to every rule,
and all that...

    azurée

~

ONCE, MY SISTER, Arshia, tried to teach me stage-fighting.
I think she just wanted the opportunity to smack me

around. As we sparred, she demanded that we always maintain eye contact. She claimed that accidents occur when we blink—when we fail to see the other person as a person. In fact, she said "blinking" is how people cope with hurting others. That idea explains her. It explains Beirut.

Arshia—there is a whole pulse of light in our sisterhood she's tried to extinguish. In Beirut, babies were born into war. For us in Québec, with different fathers, it was the same. Once, we were closer. When I would draw a bath, she would sit on the bathroom counter to keep me company. Then she'd hand me a towel to dry off, and then plunge into the leftover soapy water.

She went back home to Montreal for university. The stories she sent back... With a severe attitude, and a detached heart, one can get away with almost anything. I think she understands her place in the hierarchy of things much better than I do. An older man is just a hurdle; on the other side is what she wants. So she spread her legs and jumped, clearing it easily.

When I look at my scars, I see her. And blink.

Zaev likes to pretend he's loaded with machismo, but he just screams insecurity. The men here walk with their pelvises forward and their brains flipped backwards. Is that why the boar rammed into Tammuz? I wonder if Astarte was relieved when he died.

Zaev takes my finger and slurps it past his lips. Can he

taste the things I have touched? The roasted red pepper tahini I fed on. The saltwater Mediterranean that bellyflops along the shores of La Corniche. The menstrual blood that mottled my thighs this morning. The dust collecting at the base of the Roman ruins.

Zaev suckles. He polishes me with his tongue. Kneads with his teeth. Rotates my finger upside down, and I rub the ridges of his palate. They flow like tiny valleys, smooth and soft. I want to dance all night on the roof of his mouth. Then smash it in.

I snatch back my finger and strike him with my nails along the blunt edge of his jaw. A robust pleasure crawls through my rib cage. Want him to look back at me, at the distance between our two breathless bodies, and wrestle me down. A smackdown. A throwdown. My brain drifts away from the furor of it all.

Want him to break my clavicle. To cut me along my bone and lick the blood. My Zen is a moth that can't stop scorching itself. A moth driven crazy by flames.

I sneer, "Hit me." Repeat myself. Press my forehead up to his and exhale along the curl of his eyelashes.

He has a martyr's glare. His fingers slide up my ankles. He clutches around my heels and, with a jolt of muscle, yanks my body forward so my back smacks down on the mattress. He twists the skin along my calves, and it burns as he wrenches my legs up onto his shoulders. I can hear his belt jingling and knocking into itself as he unbuckles it. If he looks at my Zen planet, will he see the beads of pleasure there, pulsating?

There is something clinging to the inside of me, and I want him to scrape it out with his cock.

He finally enters my planet. Then he smacks me with an open palm.

"Now you're an Arab," I say. We never lose eye contact.

IV

Sent: March 3, 2006, 11:54 AM
Subject: RE: RE: RE: RE: Bénédictions
My Azurée,
On my end—big epiphany: I realized yesterday that carrying around a broken heart is exhausting. Sometimes I'm tired of my own heart. No sympathy required. It just occurred to me (I'm slow).

The loss of my wife five years ago was like a death blow to me. Now I have to face the darkness alone and I'm too old to run away in the old ways. Everything is either in recovery or disintegrating.

So, tell me about Zaev. How did you two become friends, anyway?

With love,
Matt

I sit at the internet café, arching my cunt against the plastic seat. Marking my territory. Matt's continued presence, like he owns real estate in my everyday life, makes him a cumbersome character. His wisdom isn't really wise. Why do I keep hitting reply? I just want to walk through Beirut—flowers, flies, flesh, and all—without interruptions from a man with obscene visions of being my daddy figure.

I am not my reckless sister, no matter how much I have waded into her waters. Deep water and drowning are not the same thing. I just want to look at my scars without hating myself.

Sent: March 4, 2006, 2:33 AM
Subject: RE: RE: RE: RE: RE: Bénédictions
dear matt,

you're right. everything is either in recovery or disintegrating.

it's interesting you call your wife's passing a death blow. you must have read emily dickinson. she wrote, "a death-blow is a life-blow to some, who till they died did not alive become."

you've really lived, matt. i feel like I'm in life's dress rehearsal. but if i don't like the outcome, i can still change my script. i can remove a character if he's not vital to my plot.

don't worry about zaev. he's not a story to tell. he's
an anecdote.

azurée

Climbing the stairs out of the dark basement into the
lashing waves of light and heat, my dilated pupils refuse to
adjust. I cannot stop blinking.

ZAEV ASKS IF he can keep the motor running. He leans
against the hood of his taxi, one foot crossed over the other,
his loose black pants falling over the rounded heel of his
shit-kicking boots.

I tell him to shut it off. He fidgets like bullets are ricocheting off his body. He folds and unfolds his arms over
his chest, and I can feel him watching my legs as I slink
down across the Pigeons' Rock, the only remaining natural
feature of Beirut.

The Mediterranean horizon swallows the sun like a
python. Light skips away in awkward peels, slowly dull-
ing. There is a worn path across the top of the rocks. Twin
limestone formations with the lazy sea undulating between
them. They form horseshoes over the water like Percé
Rock. I need to return to Québec.

Water sluices in raging currents and gurgles as it gets
trapped in the undertow. The skin on the bottoms of my

feet winces with the shifting pressure of my steps over sizzling flat stones and jagged rock jutting from the sporadic moss and slime. I will count the scars later.

"Salaam alaikum, ya habibti." Zaev pulls down his Ray-Bans. He shrinks as I move farther out onto the edge of the rocks.

My flight leaves in mere hours, but there's something in the rabid sun that slices through the low villas shrouded with magenta bougainvillea, in the yellow stucco buildings between cedar trees, that beckons me. I have the space to hear new things. A bed within me to burrow into. A sacred ritual like a prayer chant.

When Zaev woke up that first morning, I tugged my pink-and-red underwear out from underneath him, my fingers still sticky with hummus. He reached over and pressed his thumb into my erect nipple, trying to invert it. "One day, you will understand the calming powers of your body," he whispered at daybreak.

He was right. For a time, I wanted to be the wild Beirut boar. But I'm the one who's been punctured and buried on the mount. Quiet. Serene. Tranquil.

One day, when I stop all this fucking, I'm going to start thinking.

I'm going to point myself out in a mirror and recognize the fall of my hip, the rise of my back, the dip of my shoulder, the peak of my collarbone.

I'm going to know. That perhaps these scars were all for the best.

Now, warm gusts dance about my body as I straddle the sea. I visualize the place where the mouth of the Mediterranean tongues the Atlantic. Where the Atlantic gargles the Saint Lawrence. Where the Saint Lawrence swallows the echoes of my family as they stepped off the boat in Montreal. The shores that my great-grandmother left behind stretch before me like a matrimonial veil.

I lift up my skirt. The tide holds its breath.

RUE BERRI

2014

HELLO AND WELCOME to your audio guide to 7173 Rue Berri in Montreal. Today we will guide you through the ground-floor apartment where your Lebanese grandparents lived for many years, in the 1930s, '40s, and '50s, that you've never bothered to visit because you're so wrapped up in your carefree life in Toronto.

Today, you'll be able to explore this flat at your leisure; you can pause or rewind each section as you move through the space. To hear more about the Marché Jean Talon just down the street that you haven't set foot in since you were a whiny and insolent prepubescent, press 101. To hear more about Saint Nicholas Syrian Orthodox Church around the corner on de Castelnau—the church where your great-grandfather served as original treasurer, the church where you were baptized, and the church you now mock and lampoon in your atheist rants (no, no, no, we understand, we love Christopher Hitchens, too)—press 201.

That's not to say your family has ever been big on religion. Bunch of crooks, churches are. Sure, Sito and Jido celebrated Christmas, but that was only because your great-grandfather was a member of Saint Nick's congregation. No one in the family has ever really believed in a god.

Just call us Lebenezer Scrooge. Bah, hummus.

To get the names and phone numbers of suitable Arab bachelors who live nearby—don't worry, we know their mothers—press 301. Oh, we forgot... your feminism. We support that. But habibti, it's always good to have a man around. But what do we know? There's no charge for this audio guide, but you could call us once in a while.

You are now facing 7173 Rue Berri. Notice the winding, wrought-iron staircase curling down the front brickwork, which is a classic Montreal architectural design. You will find this feature across the Plateau, Mile End, Côte-des-Neiges, Saint-Henri, and NDG. Your mother used to sleep in the bedroom under that staircase. All she could see out her window was black iron and spliced sunshine. There are photographs of your mother as a toddler and Sito standing on that staircase. In those pictures, the sidewalk is dirt and gravel; the cars on the street are rounded and smooth.

Notice the front door—wood-framed with a stained-glass window. Do you see the initials HG in the corner?

Your jido installed that door with his bare hands. Some things were built to last. Uncle Ali lived on the second floor and would come downstairs every evening and sit with your mother, Sito, and Jido, and they'd eat crisp cherries and fresh cantaloupe slices from the Marché Jean Talon. The neighbours would sit on the stoop and play gin rummy. No one does that anymore. Do you even know your neighbours? Does the local soda jerk know you by name? Stop fiddling with your smartphone and listen.

As you enter the flat, you are greeted by a pleasant, retired Vietnamese man who has renovated most of the interior since he took possession in the 1990s. His hairline is running away from him, and he sports a tacky '90s sweater. Be polite—he has lost his wife; give him the respect he deserves. He only speaks French—have you kept up with your French? Oh, you have! Impressive. And here we thought you had become one of those maudit anglophones.

Follow him down the long front corridor. Notice the original floorboards and traces of wallpaper that he merely painted over. This is the corridor down which your mother used to roller skate when she was thirteen. You can still see the wheel marks in the varnish. The door frame and light fixtures in your mother's front bedroom are still there. You can see in this room a curtain demarcating it from the adjoining middle room where Sito and Jido used to sleep. This is now a gilt shrine to the Vietnamese man's late wife.

What religion do they practice in Vietnam? Oh, don't give us that look. You can put that face back in the garbage where you found it.

The volume on your device appears to be malfunctioning, if you cannot hear the audio, please press restart now.

Moving along, next you'll find the door leading down to the basement. In the 1940s, this was a trap door gaping through the floorboards. Here, Sito would store her stewed peaches and green-tomato ketchup in Mason jars. There were loaves of Syrian bread (Stop calling it pita bread— "pita" is a Greek word, and this bread originates in Syria, got it?) and containers of laban (salty yogourt). And on special occasions, you might have found kaak bi haleb (milk cakes) and bit'leywa (Stop calling it baklava! What did we tell you about the Greeks?). Finally, you will find the backroom, where the Vietnamese man sleeps. This was once the bedroom of your great-grandmother Alzira, whom you lovingly called Sito Number Two. Did your mother never teach you the proper Arabic word for great-grandmother? Shameful.

Follow the jovial Vietnamese man whose name escapes us at the moment (this old grey mare, she ain't what she used to be . . .) as he shows you the original features of the flat. The built-in pantry that still bears the carved edges and rounded sides indicative of 1940s craftsmanship. See how the light switches were push buttons? Electrical outlets were only two-pronged. Most kitchenware was brown-hued. Wind-up alarm clocks. Typewriters missing the return lever. Rotary phones. Mason jars full of off-white flour. Tea tins with pictures of powdered ladies on them. Large silver spoons. Tonics in little blue bottles. Chlorodyne tablets in hand-painted ivory pillboxes. The original glass cabinet built to fit inside the wall with the floral highlights and gauzed, bubbled glass remains. The forties, man. Your family left this house in the sixties to move to suburban Ville Saint-Laurent, but man... the forties.

Press 300 to close your eyes and imagine the sounds of your family's young voices in conversation, fighting, crying, kissing bruised knees, tasting sauces.

Press 302 to hear the *thack thack thack* of Jido's type-writer, the bubbly percolation of Sito's glass General Electric coffee maker, the *wooga-wooga-wooga* of your mother's skipping rope slapping the walls as she double-Dutched.

Press 303 to hear the story of how Sito and Jido met. They were at a café on Rue Belanger when Jido approached Sito sitting in a booth and said, "You I'm going to sleep with." Sito smacked him fiercely across the face. "What are you doing, you stupid broad? I'm paying you a compliment!" he said, and she replied... Oh, you haven't pressed 303 yet. We'll wait. We know you've heard the story a million times, we just thought... No, no, no, you're right, we're rambling.

Who listens to old audio guides anymore anyway? No one even calls us anymore. We might as well crawl into a corner and malfunction.

Now stand outside. Stand in the snow and stare at their front porch again. Hold up your monochrome family photos. Hold them up and try to picture a young Sito kissing a young Jido on this porch. Picture your mother, a toddler, learning to walk down this street. To learn more about how to photograph a photograph into a photograph, press 541 before your head explodes from the meta of it all.

Press 600 to speak to your jido.

You have pressed 600.

Take the #11 bus up Mount Royal. From up here, the city below is muffled by the trees, the closeness to heaven. The bus lets you off at the south entrance of Mount Royal Cemetery. There are no sidewalks, so you have to walk on the road. The scent of death is everywhere, and gravestones carry an unbearable, unendurable sadness. You haven't visited Jido since you were a little girl. The snow has submerged all the gravestones. Damned Montreal blizzards. Notorious, they are. You haven't had to endure so many centimetres since the early 1990s when you would toboggan out of your second-floor window after a storm. The front doors were blocked by the fluffy white stuff. Then you moved to Toronto and never came back.

As you walk, look for the black stone with Arabic script

along the top. It's across the road from the firemen's monument. No, no, you've gone too far. Retrace your steps; turn back. Nope, too far again. You're going to have to clean off some of the stones if you want to find Jido.

Look out across the horizon, beyond the mount's edge. See how Montreal prepares to sleep in this violet haze descending from the west. The sky looks like a melted Popsicle, and the sun will promptly set. You have to speak to Jido before nightfall, before the gates shut and darkness blinds you.

On the corner by a roundabout, do you notice the unusually high snowbank? The plows have dumped all the slush and sleet and snowy detritus onto this one corner. You will notice, peeking out from this mass, the tippy-top of a black stone. Your eyes do not deceive you. That is Arabic script across the top.

You will have to climb up and over the massive pile if you want to find Jido. You're wearing boots and mitts, c'mon now. You're a tough Canadian broad, as you're constantly reminding every man who dumps you. Surely, you can withstand a little snow. Dive in, habibti.

Oh dear, it's going up to your hips. You'll have to dig him out.

As you assume the doggie-dig position and hurl snow back and out between your legs, you will slowly reveal the black stone. Dig with all the anger and passion and frustration that has been building up in you for some time. Why did you return to Montreal anyway? Why have you come to visit us after so many years of silence? Did you love someone? Did you lose someone? Maybe it's because sometimes the only way to move forward is to look back. To see how far you've come. We understand, habibti. That kind of heartbreak can be a real roadblock. But you are always welcome home.

Keep digging—there's your great-grandfather. Your great-uncles and -aunts. The snow slowly gives way. And there is Jido at the bottom, with an engraving so fresh it could have been carved mere hours ago.

Keep the photos in your purse. Keep your camera in your back pocket. Keep the images of Sito and Jido embracing on their front porch, alive and full of vigour, in your mind. Time is a construct. Jido is waiting for you on the front porch. Go ahead, you can speak to him. He is listening to you talk about your life, which can be in such shambles sometimes. He nods with knowing eyes. He knows how deep your pain runs. He feels it in his bones. It's a family trait.

Colours shift and fade over Montreal. Your toes are ice and your spine tingles with a chill.

Atop the mount, tell Jido everything.

To hear Jido's response, press #.

YOUR HANDS ARE BLESSED

Yis Lemli Hidayki

2015

WHEN COUSIN EMIL'S WIFE, Marwan, disappeared on her way home from the university, Sito was finally persuaded to leave Damascus. The refugee camp was just over the border in Lebanon. It was already full of Syrians, but Sito recognized no friends or neighbours. There were families from Homs and Aleppo, and the more industrious ones were selling food and water. Their white tents became shops clad in sheet metal and tin. Bottles of water for one lira. The flatbreads were made with black flour, and the loaves were made with too much yeast so they would rise quickly. The soups, comprising boiled barley and beans, were made with unclean water. The meat was fermenting salami, probably goat or desert hog.

Sito had been a piano teacher all her life—what did she know of selling wares? Emil tried to show her how she might be useful. He got his hands on long needles and thin Bemberg fabric, but after years of being a concert pianist, her knuckles and joints hurt. A dull ache deep inside, as if she had slept on her hands the wrong way.

"Baladi, baladi..." she would repeat when she thought no one could hear her. *My country, my country...*

Sito and Emil were in the refugee camp for eight months before I was able to bring them to Montreal. Sponsoring them privately meant that I had to demonstrate I could cover the cost for a year, so I took out a second line of credit. My father didn't help; he wanted her with him in Sicily, but the swell of migrants in Lampedusa made it impossible. They flew into the international airport in Toronto on a Tuesday. My six-hour drive there flew by like migrating magpies. They came out of the arrival hall wearing new winter jackets. A few months earlier, our prime minister had made a big hullabaloo by personally handing out parkas, smiling with his hand over his heart. Now, there were no cameras.

The airport was white with green carpeting. Emil was pushing the valise cart, and Sito gripped his arm. She looked like a half-mast flag in the wind.

I greeted them with kisses and hugs. I was so glad to have my sito again. She used to hold me when I was an angsty teen and feed me bits of kibbeh ("Because it's good for you") in between bites of bit'leywa ("Don't tell your father"). She used to feed the birds on her back balcony, the scent from the cedar trees wafting through the air. The building's courtyard echoed the false notes of her piano students. I grew to hate Beethoven's 7th and Chopin's Nocturne in F Minor, but for some reason, not even the sloppiest student could sully Erik Satie's *Gymnopédies*.

"Ib khibic, Sito!" *I love you.*

"Ana ib khibic camaney . . ." she replied meekly. *I love you, too.*

"Siti inti helwi! Inti chatra!" *My sito is so pretty and smart.*

"Oh, knock it off, Azurée," she mumbled as we loaded the car. She refused my hand when I offered, her eyes black like a starling's.

We rode back to Montreal on a sun-dappled day. I pointed out the large Canadian flag in Joyceville, the Big Apple in Colborne, and we stopped at the Dairy Queen in Lancaster so she could have a taste of cold.

We crossed the border into Québec, and the cracked asphalt peppered with potholes made Sito's head scarf topple to her shoulders. She never pulled it back up.

EMIL WASTED NO time getting a job unloading crates at the Marché Jean Talon, so he was out the door every morning by 4:00 a.m., bless him. With just the two of us remaining, Sito and I would sit on our front porch during the quiet stillness of morning. She wanted to drink her coffee black and feed the birds. She'd never seen squirrels before, outside of American movies, and they ate all the feed and chased the swallows away. This made her laugh. She didn't understand the Montreal ritual of walking with your coffee. "Why don't they sit and drink it? Why is everyone showing off their coffee to the neighbourhood?"

"They've got to go to work, Sito. It's coffee on the go."

On the go was not something she'd ever heard of.

From the porch, every Thursday morning before garbage collection, we would watch the Chinese ladies with their shopping carts go from bin to bin, pulling out bottles and empties. Sito watched them with a hawk's eye. She didn't ask questions, even though she asked questions about everything—Why are all the stairwells on the outside of the houses here? Why do we have so many bagels in the fridge? Why do you eat maple syrup on snow? What is a Tam-Tam? Why do you swear on Catholic chalices and not Orthodox ones? Who is this Simonaque you keep mentioning?

But with the Chinese ladies, she was silent, cataloguing every nuance and detail. They dragged their wine carts behind them or pushed their shopping trollies. They wore rubber gloves and had many reusable shopping bags. They opened each blue recycling bin, and then whipped out a small flashlight no bigger than a finger. They'd tilt the bin one way, look inside, pull out the malachite bottles and brightly coloured empties, tilt the bin the other way, and again flash the light. Then one more tilt for good measure. Up and down the streets they went, putting all they found in their carts until they were full. One lady hung bags off her bicycle handles. Another woman used a rolling dolly. They came dressed for tempests, gales, and snowstorms.

Sito was transfixed. She watched as our neighbours ran out to give them their bottles with a quick hello and a smile. She noticed people across the street leaving their empties next to the bins so the ladies didn't have to dig.

The ladies each had their turf, too. West of Saint-Urbain was this lady's; east of Saint-Laurent was that lady's. No going north of Van Horne for this lady; no going south of Laurier for the other. Mile End was evenly divided.

Our side of the street belonged to June. I didn't know much about June. Her French wasn't great, but she could make herself understood. If I'm being honest, I liked June. She didn't bother me with chit-chat, and she didn't rattle my bins as loudly as the other ladies. She was to the point, and I salute that kind of dedication. Leaving her my empties was a pleasure. Sometimes I would find a pecan tart on my stoop with a note: *Merci!—de June*. Another time, six sparkling Christmas ornaments. Foaming hand soap that smelled like a vanilla candle. She did the same for my neighbours. Alexandre next door got two new colouring books for his girls. Frédérique on the corner got an osmanthus flower cake.

∽

AFTER A WHILE, Sito wanted to spend her mornings going for a walk, so she offered to get us coffees every day from the Haddad Sisters, a Lebanese bakery down the street. If everyone did a "coffee walk," she might as well do what the Montréalais do. And at least at the Haddad Sisters' she could speak Arabic.

She was always an early riser, like 5:45, so I left money on the credenza for her. By the time I'd get up around 7:15, she'd be sitting at the dining room table with our coffees and some sfiha for us to nibble on.

One morning I was up at 6:15. My thoughts were rolling around in my head, festering and rotting. Things weren't great with Sullivan since Sito came. How was I supposed to see him? He couldn't come here now, and I could hardly sneak away to his place. He was frustrated but also understanding and gentle, which made things even worse. If he had been an incomprehensible and unmitigated ass, a breakup would have been easy. But no, he had to be sensible and kind.

When I got out of bed and went to the dining room, Sito wasn't back from the Haddad Sisters. And she still wasn't back by 6:30. Or by 6:45.

"Did you get lost?" I asked her when she finally strolled in with a tray of coffee and sfiha.

She had quietly locked the door behind her but jumped at the sound of my voice. Surprised to see me awake and standing in the corridor, she looked at me like she was fresh out of things to say.

SULLIVAN PULLED ME aside one day in the break room.

"No," I whispered. "I thought we agreed never to do this here."

"Don't worry, just a friendly hello from a work buddy." He smiled as he poured himself a coffee from the slow-drip and topped mine up. "Where's your head at these days?"

"I'm sorry, I know, I've really been absent."

Sullivan had this way of making me apologize without ever even expressing hurt. He sipped from his mug and kept his eyes on the warehouse floor just beyond the break room windows. The home and garden centre team was watering the strawberry plants, and the plumbing and electrical experts were guiding DIY-ers to the nozzles and plugs aisle. Working here reminded me of my father.

"I used to think at times I could read your mind," he said into his mug, our eyes never meeting. "But now, it's..."

"It's Sito," I said. "I think she's trying to pull a fast one."

"She's your grandmother, not a moody teen."

I snorted. "You don't know her. She's sneaking away every morning."

He put the mug down, wiped his hands on the back of his reflective vest, and reached for my hand. "Well, if she's sneaking away, maybe you could, too?" His hand was clammy and callused.

Slipping out of his palm, I walked briskly back to the power tool section.

WAITING FOR SITO to come home each morning made me develop a strange relationship with my living room. I came to know each crevice and crack, and watched them expand and contract with the passing hours. I washed the floors again and again, and stepped on them too soon in socks. I cried on the couch while my cat consoled me. I cooked too much oatmeal. Even ate it, too. I formed an unbreakable bond with yogourt. I dreamed of hosting dinner parties with dear friends, introducing them to Sito and Sullivan, and being comfortable with that. The ticking clock on the wall mocked me. *Who do you think you are?* it asked.

ONE AFTERNOON ON his day off, I sat with Emil as tears, like peach blossoms, fell from his eyes.

"I never loved anyone like I loved Marwan." His lower lip trembled and his chin collapsed.

All this time, he had been holding out hope that she was in another refugee camp. Maybe she was injured and lost her memory. Maybe she'd find her way back to Emil. A new life in Montreal was so close for them both. But after many inquiries with the UNHCR, that was looking less likely.

"Why did I let her walk alone?" he berated himself. "Why didn't I walk with her?"

"Knowing Marwan, she would have shooed you away," I said. "She was too proud for an escort."

Emil hung his head like a swaying ornament, but then he started to nod. "I should have followed her. I'd have all the answers to my questions if I'd just stayed a few metres behind her."

I wanted to hold his hand, but he balled it into a fist. I covered it with my palm, as he watched the swallows migrating across the sky beyond the window.

I WAS BEHIND the wheel of my car, sitting on my cold hands and waiting for Sito to emerge. I had set my alarm and slipped out of the house unnoticed. When she finally came out the front door, she paused on the porch to tie her head scarf under her chin like a kerchief. She hadn't worn a head scarf around me since the drive from Toronto, but now, she slowly took the porch steps down to the sidewalk and, pulling a slim wine cart behind her, walked up the street, her head scarf like armour.

I put the car into gear. When she passed the turn for the Haddad Sisters, and stopped on the sidewalk to chat briefly with June, I pulled the car over. Sito walked to the side of a house, opened the recycling bin, tipped it this way and that, pulled out three cans and two green bottles, loaded her wine cart, and wiped her hands on the brim of the windbreaker I had given her.

I sat in my car for a long time, engine off, gripping the wheel until my knuckles were ivory-plated and the dry skin cracked. Sito disappeared up one side of the street, reappearing down the other. I called Sullivan, but there was no answer.

Sito slipped down a side alleyway to the next street. Following her on foot, I watched as she popped into the local SAQ. June and some of the other women were already there. Through the window, I saw her disappear into the rear of the shop behind the racks of Italian and French wine, headed for the bottle return.

When I got back to my car, Sullivan had texted. *Was sleeping.* The hot tears bloomed, brimmed, and fell like stones.

When Sito came home, I was sitting on the porch. Her head scarf was down about her shoulders.

"Habibti," she said to me like a question. "Look."

She reached down into the wine cart that had a faint boozy stench and pulled out a lemon sugar cake wrapped in cellophane. She held it like she was cupping a sparrow.

"Did you get that at the Haddad Sisters?" I asked.

She sat next to me and placed the cake on her lap. "Would you like a slice?"

Nodding to her, I rubbed my hands together, the only thing keeping me from talking more. The lemon cake was moist and still warm, with a hint of za'atar spice, cloves, and lemon zest. Crumbs fell into the ends of my hair.

The money I had left her for coffee sat untouched on the credenza, and were I to question her further, she would have no choice but to tell me everything. *I know*, I could say, *what you're doing. If you needed extra money, why didn't you just ask me?*

But I didn't say anything. Because I couldn't.

We sat silently as the sky turned from a hazy salmon to bright linseed, eating our cake.

"Montreal is a fine city," Sito said after a while.

My hands folded in my lap, almost as if they were praying.

MABROUK

2020

THE CAFÉ ON de Gaspé has a fixie bicycle hanging from the ceiling, and the barista has tattoos crawling up her back. Azurée is exhausted after another night spent on the chesterfield. The pour-over coffee slowly cools in her mug, untouched as she sits in the window and reads. The paper is filled with news from China and Italy about a virus from bats that is spreading and killing humans. Italians are singing opera from their balconies in quarantine. Drones chase children in China until they return home. The espresso machine whirs as Azurée reads—now about a local cargo shipwreck, stuck in the Lachine Canal.

Fingers inky, she leaves prints on the mug as a headline catches her eye. "A PIONEER AND PROVOCATEUR: PERFORMANCE ARTIST ULAY DIES." Azurée blinks; she knows that name from somewhere. Some viral video where two former lovers, now ravaged by age and time, sit opposite one another in chairs, not having seen each other for over twenty years. Tearfully, they reach for each other.

Reading on, the sun slicing through the plate glass window, she learns the dead artist and his lover commemorated the end of their relationship by walking from opposite ends of the Great Wall of China, where today a virus wafts through the air and steals people's lungs. The dead artist began his hike in the Gobi Desert, and his Serbian lover set out from the Yellow Sea. After thousands of kilometres, they met in the middle, the height of the wall rendering them giants above the rolling hills below. The dead artist held his lover close as she cried, the glow of dusk reflecting off their cheeks. They never saw each other again, until the chairs. And now the artist is dead.

As Azurée climbs the exterior stairwell to her second-floor brownstone on Laurier Ouest, thinking about this story, she can hear Malik's music. "I Can Never Go Home Anymore" by the Shangri-Las. When she opens the door, he is whipping up some lentil and rice dish on the stovetop. The smell of allspice and cumin is louder than the stereo.

"Hey," he mumbles, seeing her kick off her flats, but quickly returns to his boiling pot.

"Hey," she replies, shoving her hands in her pockets.

"How was..." he trails off.

"Oh, good," she jumps in. "Good, good, good."

"Good," he repeats. His wooden spoon splatters sauce

onto the counter, narrowly missing his shirt, and he jumps back.

"How was your…"

"Mezzo-mezzo." He snaps off the element, puts a lid on the pot, and wipes his hands on the back of his jeans.

They stand facing each other from across the room—her with one foot in the living room, him with one foot out of the kitchen—but it might as well be kilometres. She allows herself one glance at the hollow curve of collarbone up to his neck; that was her secret place once.

This is the most they've spoken to each other in two weeks. Since the big blowout. He knew about the scars— hell, he'd traced his fingers over them many times. But it turns out he wasn't as comfortable with them as he congratulated himself he was. She had cried and called him names. He yanked at his hair like her words were driving him bonkers. Doors were slammed. Plates broken. She's been picking shards out of her heels for days.

She's looking, obviously, but there are no three-and-a-halfs in her budget on the market right now. After Sito passed and Cousin Emil remarried, she sold the big, old house in Little Italy, so there is no going home again. She moved in with Malik not long after, a happy time she doesn't dare think about now. So in the meantime they do this little dance, avoiding each other around the apartment as much as possible. She's suddenly a coffee drinker, though she secretly hates the stuff. He's so busy at the office most nights, whereas he never once stayed at work beyond dinnertime before.

It's torture, this awkwardness. *I've had more enjoyable pap smears*, she thinks.

The song ends, and now it's "He Hit Me (It Felt Like a Kiss)" by the Crystals.

She pulls the clipped newspaper obit from her jeans pocket. "I read something interesting today," she says, as he wipes down the granite counter. Moving toward him, she can see him stiffening up.

"Here." She hands him the story about Ulay. He gives her a look before reading.

"I was thinking," she continues, unsure of her words, "maybe before I go, we could do this."

He looks at her like the answer to the question brewing in his head is written on her face. His jaw clenches and releases.

"Where to?"

AZURÉE FOLDS A paper plane and tries to make it fly. When she was in grade one, the older kids taught her to aim for the back wall and point the plane straight ahead, not up or down, so it can loop and swoop. But it's been years, and the paper plane nosedives at her feet. She's embarrassed, but not even the bartender has noticed. No one is ever as concerned with her failures as she is.

This is the bar in the Saint-Henri neighbourhood where she and Malik once drank and played a card game while everyone else folded and fumbled with their paper planes. The bar hands out the paper planes with every drink—a cute gimmick to keep people drinking. That night, Azurée and Malik ended up talking to this elderly couple seated on the bar stools next to them and they played cards all night.

Azurée is starting in the west of town. Ouest.

Malik is starting east. He's beginning at the tip of Île Sainte-Hélène, where last autumn they tried to go skinny-dipping at dusk but found the water too unseasonably freezing.

Now, during the first flush of March, he swims in the icy cold tide until his breath is a pain inside, his arms are heavy, and the masts on the boats in the Saint Lawrence look like naked trees against the sky. Most masts are bare, with only swinging ropes for adornment, but one that passes under the Cartier Bridge looks like a giant cabbage moth has set upon it.

Diving into freezing water is an entire thing now, named after a Dutch man called Wim Hof who preaches that cold water resets our bodies and minds. Legions of postulants flock to social media to post videos of their attempts. Over the past couple weeks, Malik has converted. Cold showers three times a day. He figures this swim is just a way to step up his game.

For almost a moment, he thinks Azurée was on that boat passing beneath the bridge, her arms outstretched, rising above the water line, offering to pluck him, dripping and shivering, from the currents.

It must be her, he thinks, *because she's carved out of wood.*

AZURÉE STOPS AT the McDonald's parking lot in Griffintown that looks down the slope to the Atwater Market. One night, a long time ago, she and Malik brought badminton rackets to this lot and slapped a shuttlecock back and forth over a concrete divider. It was one of those hot and sticky nights when the asphalt is still warm and it's late enough into the hush of night that a busy intersection is uncharacteristically still. They raced each other across the lot, keeping the shuttlecock floating and soaring above their heads.

Malik tripped and scraped his knee—bits of gravel and pebbles embedded in his torn flesh. He winced as she delicately pulled them out, blowing lightly to cool the burn. She kissed the white, dead skin hanging from his scrape.

"I love you," he told her.

It was the first of firsts. The beginning of everything. She had never loved another Arab before, especially not a

Syrian like her father. All the men before had been versions of white.

They returned to that parking lot often, always after dark, when all that glowed in the ambrosial moonlight was a border of dewy grass. The surrounding houses and cafés were quiet. Damselflies flitted over the humming crickets. They'd amble slowly through the gravel and stones of the lot after hours, exchanging colourful puns for a bazillion food/movie title mash-ups.

"*Great Scrambled Eggspectations*," she said.

Pause.

"*Mars A-tacos*," he replied.

Long pause.

"*There's Something about Calamari.*"

Pause.

"*Silence of the Leg of Lamb.*"

Pause.

"*Dude, Where's My Carpaccio?*"

"Only you would think of that," he guffawed.

"I know, right."

Long pause.

"*Raiders of the Lost Artichoke.*"

Pause.

"*Stand by Meatloaf.*"

"Ooh, wait. How about *There Will Be Bloody Marys*?" he laughed.

"Ha! Okay, um..."

"This is hard."

"It really is!" she exclaimed. "Wait, I got one. *Die Hard Boiled Eggs.*"

"Corny!"

"All right, come on, Einstein."

Pause.

"A Few Good Mango Salads."

The giggles consumed them. This spot of so much action and fury during the day was a private area for them.

Now, the car exhaust and the piercing, tinny sound of the drive-thru speaker move her along.

She makes her way to the mountain, climbing the series of steps from the corner of Peel and Pine, up to the Belvedere lookout. The old chalet behind the lookout is cavernous and cold. The trees are quiet sentries, and dogs yip and slobber at their owners to hurry up.

Last Halloween, she and Malik climbed up to the lookout at midnight, wearing sparkly silver capes borrowed from their five-year-old neighbour. They watched the moon pass over the Cartier, the Victoria, and the Champlain Bridges, flashing brilliant upon the iron suspensions. The moon was so large that night nothing could turn it upside down.

Azurée listens to the pounding against her ear drums. A thumping, like a heart that can't keep the beat.

~

AS MALIK DRIES OFF, the downbeat of Piknic Électronik calls out to him. It's normally a summer rave in the woods, but with lockdowns and quarantines spreading from city to city, this little rave seems to be unofficial, unticketed, and just for those who might be in earshot. He feels the bass reverberating and ricocheting off his bones. Last year, he and Azurée danced together, shaking their bodies like they could fling off their arms and legs and ascend to heaven as angels.

Malik gets off the Metro at Pie-IX. The Stade Olympique with the retractable roof built for the 1976 Olympics dominates the sky before him. Famously, the roof wasn't finished in time for Bruce Jenner to break the world record in the decathlon, or Nadia Comăneci to earn a perfect ten in gymnastics. Malik knows this because everyone's Montreal taxes are paying for the stadium...still. It was here that he and Azurée once dared each other to walk the entire length of the stadium grounds while remaining totally silent. No words, just body language to communicate. He was damned if he was going to speak first, and she behaved as if she had taken a vow of silence. They walked and walked— past the stadium, across the busy street to the botanical gardens, and the entire length of that, too—smiling and trying to provoke the other to speak first. Her eyes told him she would win. His replied, *In a pig's eye*. She tried to poke him in the ribs to cheat a sound out of him. He chased after her, past the hostas and birds of paradise, all the way to the African violets and Turkish hanging gardens.

After hours, they walked to the nearest bike share stand, where he finally said, "You win."

"You're a huge tampon!" she gloated.

Now Malik walks this entire distance again, without even the pleasure of her silence for company. He puts in his earbuds, and the first song on the playlist is the Shirelles' "Will You Still Love Me Tomorrow."

AZURÉE CLIMBS TREES in Parc Jarry, where the Expos used to train. She makes a pinhole camera at a workshop inside the Station 16 Gallery on the Main, and goes up to every mural, snapping them on thirty-five-millimetre film. She even goes down to the Lachine Canal near the Farine Five Roses factory to look at the industrial container shipwreck that's run aground in the water before it gets towed off to the coast.

She intended for this exercise to pay homage to their love, but if she's being honest with herself, she was hoping this tour through the ephemeral moments of their relationship might trigger something. Some buried emotion. Some last-minute change of heart. Some deep-seated need for each other.

Last year, as they lay huddled under the sheets one morning, she told Malik about Craig and Justin, the boys in Toronto who used to bully her.

"When you were born, God thought your face was your cunt, so he put hair all over it," they told her. She did everything she could to blend in, plucking her eyebrows until they looked like the square root symbol. Upon hearing that, Malik went straight to the long stretch of alleyways that run parallel with the Main, and next to a huge mural, he spray-painted, *Her Brows Were All It Took*. She had never felt more seen.

She hopes, as she sits on a bench facing the shipwreck, that Malik's playing putt-putt at the Jardin du Gamelins festival. Or that he's remembering the time they pretended to be newlyweds house hunting near the Marché Jean Talon, arguing in front of the real estate agent about where to put the nursery.

It was on this very bench, years ago, that she told him about his drunken antics the night before. It was in the early days of their courtship, and they hadn't even shared a bed yet, but one night they got too drunk at a bar on Fairmount and he made an epic, intimate move.

"You tried to kiss me on the forehead," she told him over cups of coffee, trying to shake off the hangover.

"I did?" He seemed shocked.

"Yes."

"Where."

"On my temple. A few times."

"Were you terrified?"

"No."

"What did I do after that?"

"You fell asleep."

"Did you like it?"

"How can I answer that?"

"As best you can."

"I was too drunk to mind."

"So you would have been bothered if you were sober?"

"It wouldn't have happened if we were both sober."

"All I remember is feeling your hands and asking if I could make your belly button talk by squishing it together."

"Did I let you?"

"You said I could, but I think I just fell asleep with my hand on your stomach. What kind of forehead kisses were they?"

"Malik…"

"What?"

"Do you have to draw this out?"

"I can stop."

"They were normal. Why does it matter?"

"Because I only remember telling you that I had a coupon for cuddles, snuggling up to you, and playing with your hands. No kisses. I've never kissed anybody on the forehead."

"Why not?"

"Actually, maybe I have and they just didn't tell me... until now."

Now, as Malik appears from behind her shoulder and sits next to her on the bench, Azurée can tell there will be no more forehead kisses.

The industrial container shipwreck with the word EVERGREEN emblazoned across the side cuts through the waves that crash against its hull. It is early dusk before a pair of tugboats appears and latch onto it to tractor it out to sea.

Sitting so close to him, she looks over at the nook of his neck that she so often dozed in, when Sunday mornings seemed endless. She loved to feel his carotid artery throbbing against her temple. Each pulse and palpitation was like a trophy—so much so, she often felt like he was awarding her. Congratulating her. She nicknamed the nook "the mabrouk" for that very reason. To her, his body was a blessing, a benediction.

The shipwreck finally begins to disappear behind the Farine Five Roses factory. They watch it go in silence. In the Ulay obit, the artist's Serbian lover was quoted as saying, "We never stop loving silently those we once loved out loud."

The sky turns hazy colours with a misty texture. It looks like it might collapse on them as it grows darker with the early dusk of March.

"Are you cold?" Malik asks.

She nods, and he puts his arm around her. She doesn't dare rest her head on his shoulder; she might catch the scent of the mabrouk. A couple walking on the boardwalk behind them coughs. The wife tells the man to cover his mouth before he infects her, too.

"Don't worry," the husband replies as they walk out of earshot. "It won't kill you."

It's the time of year when everyone longs for the end of winter. The cold stings like a nettle. The time that makes us long for solutions, as if they could be found in the nooks and lines of our flesh.

ACKNOWLEDGEMENTS

SOME STORIES IN this collection were previously published in alternate versions. "The Power of the Dog" was first published as "Nylon-Encased Flesh" in the Diaspora Dialogues anthology *TOK 1: Writing the New Toronto*. "A Degree of Suffering Is Required" was first published in the *Malahat Review*, Issue 153, Winter 2005. "Blink" was first published as "My Tryst with Sins" in *Descant*, Issue 145, June 2009. "Rue Berri" was first published in *subTerrain*, Issue 72, Winter 2016. "Your Hands Are Blessed" was first published in *Prairie Fire*, Fall 2021, Volume 42, No. 3. It was then republished in the Biblioasis anthology *Best Canadian Stories 2023*.

I gratefully acknowledge financial assistance for crafting and creating this book from the Ontario Arts Council, the Toronto Arts Council, and the Canada Council for the Arts.

Many of the stories in this book were directly inspired by the lives of my family and my ancestors. I hear your voices in my veins; you will not be forgotten.

I am indebted to many people for their continued support, enthusiasm, and confidence. I owe an enormous debt to Chris Bucci of Aevitas Creative Management for sticking with me all these years, for his keen eye for detail, and for walking me through the basics. An additional debt is owed to everyone at House of Anansi, most especially former publisher Leigh Nash and editor Shirarose Wilensky, who believed in this book before I did and whose countless insights gave this book its shape. Additional thanks to Meaghan Ogilvie for providing her stunning and striking photography. Special thanks to my mother, Joan Zarbatany, for supporting me in pursuit of this bonkers vocation, and for sharing stories of our family, which informed this book. The largest thanks goes to Gabriele Mabrucco for reading all my drafts, and for all the "gugs," fist bumps, and forehead kisses. Without all these people, this book could not exist.

© Panther Sohi

CHRISTINE ESTIMA is an Arab woman of mixed ethnicity (Lebanese, Syrian, and Portuguese) whose essays and short stories have appeared in the *New York Times*, *The Walrus*, *VICE*, the *Globe and Mail*, the *Toronto Star*, *Chatelaine*, *Maisonneuve*, and many more. She was shortlisted for the 2023 Lee Smith Novel Prize and the 2018 Allan Slaight Prize for Journalism, longlisted for the 2015 CBC Creative Nonfiction prize, and a finalist for the 2011 Writers' Union of Canada Short Prose Competition. Born in Trois-Rivières, she lives in Toronto.